the AVENGERS™

A Novel by
Julie Kaewert

Based on The Original Screenplay

Written by
Don Macpherson

Inspired by the classic television series,
The Avengers

TITAN BOOKS

THE AVENGERS
ISBN 1 85286 931 3

Published by
Titan Books
42-44 Dolben Street
London SE1 0UP

First edition August 1998
10 9 8 7 6 5 4 3 2 1

Titan edition published by arrangement with Bantam Books, a division of
Bantam Doubleday Dell Publishing Group, Inc.

Printed and bound in Great Britain by Cox & Wyman Ltd, Reading, Berkshire.

Prologue

In the dark recesses of Sir August de Wynter's lab at Hallucinogen Hall, the master himself stood over a clear glass tub, surrounded by phials of multicolored chemicals. Bailey, Sir August's assistant, nervously followed his master's instructions and plucked a frighteningly vivid green concoction from the rack of test tubes.

He did his best to hide his distaste for the task; Sir August was nothing if not volatile, and it wouldn't do to set him off. Nonetheless, Bailey blanched as he poured the fluid into the clear, round tub that always reminded him of a liquid womb. He'd been hired to intimidate Sir August's enemies and perform certain other unsavory tasks, which he enjoyed very much. It was every sociopath's dream to actually be *paid* to hurt other people! But playing Igor to Sir August's Frankenstein hadn't been mentioned in his contract.

Bailey prided himself on being a ruthless blighter, with all the sensitivity of a crowbar. But when he was required to come to this lab he avoided thinking about who—or rather, what—floated inside the tub. "It," as he decided the thing could only be called, gave him the creeps. It was a curvaceous female body, which was not in itself so bad, but it floated naked, suspended in that disgustingly viscous fluid. And it was wrapped in a body-hugging rubber shroud that reminded him of cling film. It was so strangely human, and yet not. . . .

"Reset genetic codes. Reactivate," Sir August ordered, sounding impatient.

Bailey flipped a switch on the adjacent control board, and immediately the sound of humming power filled the lab. The Cambridgeshire rates people had long since given up trying to work out how the mad scientist Sir August de Wynter was using up such vast amounts of power in his country home. Bailey sneered at the thought. If they only knew . . .

Sir August prodded him in the back, and he remembered himself. His smile faded. Selecting a quart container of yellow liquid, which he knew to be the next and final step in the sequence, he poured it carefully into the tub. This was the part he hated most. The thing began to wriggle like a tadpole, which was disconcerting to see in a perfect female form. Her entire body undulated rhythmically, sensually, as if she were moving to some music that only she could hear. Bailey felt himself reacting to it, then caught himself. *It's just a thing,* he told himself, revolted at the thought of being attracted to something about as human as a fish, or a frog.

"What a dreadful waste of technology," Sir August pronounced as he watched the writhing female form coming to life, sounding a bit disappointed. "Pity about the eyes . . . and . . . er . . . the other things."

Sir August, or Dr. Frankenstein, as Bailey thought of

him down here, smiled sadly at him and made some adjustments himself to the dials on the control panel.

"But those stupid fools will never even know. . . ."

Bailey was thankful that Sir August always took the final step himself. He dreaded the day when he would be asked to do it. Sir August stepped closer to the tub and reached in, peeling back the rubber shroud with reverence. Bailey found himself looking at the face of a woman who was actually quite attractive. In fact, she looked rather like the portrait of Emma Peel in Sir August's library, Bailey thought. But then her eyes popped open, and despite himself, he jumped. Grimacing, he looked her full in the face. Her eyes glinted dangerously, betraying her inhumanity. Her irises were an eerie shade of yellow.

Sir August seemed oblivious now to her defects. He leaned over the tub with solicitude and spoke pleasantly to the woman-thing. "Get up, my dear. I've another little job for you. . . ."

Bailey shivered.

CHAPTER ONE

'Tis a villain, sir, I do not love to look on.
The Tempest, *William Shakespeare*

Very few people indeed knew why the red phone box
stood in the middle of the disused airstrip. And that
was precisely the way the Ministry wanted it.

Government psychologists, defense strategists, and
security specialists had devoted months of rigorous study
to the question of how best to camouflage the entrance
to a highly dangerous, top-secret, underground government laboratory. Literally tons of paper, thousands of
printer toner cartridges, boxloads of rich tea biscuits,
and oceans of tea had been consumed considering the
issue.

At last, Britain's best minds had reached a consensus.
What could possibly be more ordinary than a phone box?
Its cherry-red color, paned windows, and raised crown
communicated comfort, tradition, and respectability—
the very thing to hide a secret program with the potential

to destroy the world. Lovely bit of irony, that, the scientists thought.

But even as they came to the end of their brilliant analysis, the government scientists knew that the phone box couldn't protect the project from spies and saboteurs. They were right about that, too.

For one day not so long ago in England, a speeding vehicle intruded on the quiet landscape of the abandoned airstrip—and the red phone box. At first the car was detectable only by a puff of smoke on the horizon and the throaty growl of high-geared acceleration; then a long, elegant Jaguar E-type streamed into view, speeding like a bullet. The car's muscular curves deflected the air for maximum efficiency, its whining engine at full throttle as it neared the phone box. Screeching to a halt, the car stirred up a blizzard of dust, which settled slowly as the silence resumed.

The delicate pop of the driver's side door opening again broke the silence of the quiet July day, and a black leather boot emerged, heavily encrusted with buckles and straps. The boot crunched into the ground as the rest of a tall, lithe woman clad entirely in black leather leapt out of the car. She was perhaps in her late twenties, and sported a long mane of thick auburn hair. A black leather catsuit clung to her long, smooth-muscled frame like a second skin.

It revealed every inch of long legs, and strong thighs that tapered into an enticingly curvaceous posterior. Buckles and tightly drawn black leather straps accentuated the narrow curves at her wrists and ankles; a long zipper of exaggerated size down her front begged to be unzipped. Tossing her reddish-brown hair the woman thrust her hip against the car door, closing it with a neat *snick*.

She strode across to the phone box, her step light. Inside, the phone had begun to ring—the polite double ring so characteristic of the British Empire. She opened the door of the box and picked up the receiver. Without seeming to move her lips, she said, "How now brown cow?" She blinked, pausing for a moment before continuing. They would expect it. "The quick brown fox jumped over the lazy dog."

Voice identification. Her voice was well known to the computer.

The woman heard a whir as the ceiling-mounted security camera behind her came to life. Swiveling her head automatically, she looked back into the lens. The camera clicked, dutifully recording the distinctive leather, the auburn hair, the flashing eyes.

From the receiver in her hand came a muffled woman's voice. "Password affirmative. Press button 'B.' "

She replaced the receiver and hung a cardboard notice on the outside of the box: "Out of Order." She grinned and stuck out an elegant finger to jab a button near the coin slot on the old Bakelite telephone. A smooth hum reverberated as the floor of the phone box slowly began to lower the leather-clad woman into the ground.

She was in.

The woman descended on the lift platform, arms folded, foot tapping impatiently, staring at the ceiling that slid into place above her. After several moments her extraordinary ride came to a stop in a sterile, high-tech-looking research lab. The lab looked and felt as it always had: cold steel walls, air locks between corridors, intensely bright recessed ceiling lighting, and the hush of a church sanctuary.

She immediately stepped off the platform and strode past an assistant, not acknowledging his smile or greeting. These fools . . . she had no time today for such absurd social rituals. She felt his eyes on her back as she continued down the long steel corridor. A shiny metal door loomed ahead, labeled: "Prospero Program—Authorized Personnel Only." Beneath the words a black-bottomed cloud was pierced by a bolt of brilliant yellow lightning—the Prospero logo. She strode purposefully toward the door.

Over an intercom, a calm male voice said, "Prospero Program, phase five. Weather conditions alpha-one. Wind speed zero-five. Cloud patterns favorable."

The woman opened the door, stepped confidently through it. A kindly looking, bespectacled man with a professorial appearance recognized her immediately. Smiling, he greeted her from across the room. "Ah, Dr. Peel. What a pleasant surprise."

She didn't acknowledge him as she entered the room, intent on moving quickly through it today and directly to her destination. With a nervous frown, the bookish little man scuttled over to meet her, then backed away again—he saw that she was prepared to walk right over him if he didn't move.

"I—I didn't expect you," he said. "I must have confused our schedule. We . . ."

She moved past him, still not bothering to answer. He hurried after her through the room and into the next corridor. The idiotic man trailed behind her hesitantly, unsure how to approach his normally civil—even urbane—colleague. She knew from the man's step, and his reaction to her earlier, that he was flummoxed. He didn't find her as witty or friendly as she normally was, or as charismatic. Well, he wouldn't be troubled by it for long. She'd see to that.

Dr. Peel lengthened her stride and continued down the corridor of shiny, scientifically sterile steel, followed by the birdlike little man. The steel-tipped heels on her boots made a *tick*ing sound on the steel with each step, the noise bouncing maddeningly from floor to wall to ceiling and back again.

But she'd *had* to wear her favorite boots today to celebrate the fulfillment of her dream. Besides, she felt *different* in them. . . . She looked up, feeling the thrill of imminent violence course through her. The halogen spotlights in the ceiling made everything shine in a most attractive way. She tossed her head, knowing that this kind of light brought out the highlights in her hair.

When at last she stopped at the first air lock, she wasted no time in opening the hatchway into the next chamber, spinning the wheel to open the air lock with precise, but manic speed. She stepped through it, leaving it open behind her with uncharacteristic insouciance. She heard the ineffectual little man still scurrying after her. In the hesitancy of the professor's footsteps, she could read his thoughts. *Most unlike Dr. Peel,* he was thinking, as he stepped through the hatchway and fell behind to close it himself.

Twice more she arrived at air locks, and again, opened them and moved steadfastly on into further sealed chambers, the clicking of her heels as consistent as a background rhythm. She let the scurrying professor close the air lock hatches after her as she proceeded through the steel labyrinth, always staring straight ahead. She would not be deterred from her goal.

The professor hurried anxiously alongside her now, casting the occasional worried glance at his colleague. She could feel his unease. *Something decidedly odd about Dr. Peel today . . .*

A countdown began from the loudspeaker. "Ten . . . nine . . . eight . . ." Dr. Peel made no acknowledgment.

Now openly worried, the professor glanced at her again as he struggled to keep up with her. "Are you all right, Dr. Peel?"

She continued to ignore him, feeling the strength in her legs as she walked. The little weasel. How had she ever put up with him?

"I've only just finished the analysis," he said with sycophantic sibilance. "One microgram of antimatter will bring the cloud storms bang on target—"

As she stood at the final air lock, she could imagine the professor frowning. She heard him say, in a troubled voice, "But, Dr. Peel—only the control room is down there, and—"

The woman swiveled, her eyes narrowed, pinning him. It was time.

"*This* way, Dr. Peel . . ." He indicated that she should return the way they had come, but hesitated. His now sweaty brow was furrowed, revealing his certainty that something was badly wrong. "Dr. Peel—?"

Without warning, she slammed him up against the stainless steel wall. When he began to slide slowly to the floor, stunned, she delivered an efficient and fatal karate chop to his neck. His death was instantaneous. He slid to the floor with a soft thud as she pulled a heavy bunch of keys, consisting of strange, cylindrical shapes, out of his pocket. Moving away, she turned purposefully toward the corridor marked "NO ACCESS: TURN BACK: DANGER! RESTRICTED."

She pushed open the doors and headed down the corridor.

A security officer, sipping tea in Prospero Program headquarters, picked her up on his monitor. In midcup, he stopped, then set down his brew of orange pekoe. It looked like Dr. Peel, but what was she . . . ? Policy was clear. He had to issue the warning, even if it was Dr. Peel, of all people. . . .

The guard found his voice and flipped the button on the intercom microphone. He spoke urgently, quietly. "Intruder in sector nine. Repeat. Intruder in sector nine. Activate security procedures."

In the control room, she carefully observed her surroundings. She stopped suddenly as she swung through the door, her lips twisted in pleasure. For a moment she stared, mesmerized, into the huge glass bubble before her. The experimental weather bubble had the appearance of a grossly oversized chemistry flask, with a violent reaction taking place inside. This, she thought, was what Prospero was all about. . . .

The control room was airtight and made of solid steel, like the others, to contain a potential runaway reaction. But it was by far the largest room in the facility, as it accommodated the storm bubble. The room was at least two stories tall, and was bisected by a steel gantry that allowed closer access to the bubble. She ran to the gantry, a scaffolding assembled from perforated metal that looked not unlike a power station tower with protrusions. With a delighted gaze upward, she swung up the stairs two at a time until she was at second-story height.

Stepping out onto the platform toward the bubble, she touched the glass with her hands and peered inside. Weather storms fizzed and crackled with maniacal force on the other side of the bubble. Black clouds spat rain, lightning bolts flashed, hurricane winds blew, mushroom clouds spouted gases—amid a snarling, raging cacophony that thrilled her to the core. She ran her hands sensually down the dangerously tight leather on her thighs, and back up again.

Over the intercom came a voice: "Radio transmitter on. Weather antenna on. Code systems, cloud sensors on."

She turned back to her work. She couldn't allow herself to be distracted. Swinging down from the gantry, she advanced rapidly to the control area. It was a long, narrow steel worktop festooned with dials, switches, monitors and indicator lights. She kicked a rolling chair out of her way. Who could sit at a time like this? With the professor's keys she unlocked the protective covers on the instrument control devices, the slightest flutter of excitement in her hand as she thought of the power she was about to unleash.

She had practiced the procedure many times. First, she used the keys to unlock the control panel; then she could start the storm. She quickly turned the keys that would enable activation of the main control switch. Her fingers twitched as she caressed the primary control lever, then thrust it upward to the On position. This was it!

She grasped the antimatter dial and began to ratchet up the amount of the volatile elements to be injected into the weather globe. Red warning lights flashed on at eye level on the control boards just as she'd known they would, then flickered urgently as she pushed the dial to its maximum setting.

An alarm began to wail; she groaned. She was breathing hard now, her heart pounding. Lights flashed warnings all round her as she twisted the antimatter injection dial ever further, her lips compressed in determination. Her eyes flicked to the temperature gauge as the needle soared into a red-painted zone. *Yes!* With a last twist, she pushed the dial past the red Danger mark.

The piercing wail of the alarm reverberated deliciously through the underground lab. Those vibrations . . . the urgency, the thrill . . . ! She hadn't dared to hope that this would be so rewarding . . . at least not in *this* way.

Over the intercom, a voice said, "Intruder alert! Intruder alert! Antimatter levels too high. Security and autodestruct procedures activated. Repeat, autodestruct activated."

In front of her, digital numbers reconfigured wildly, streams of red spinning numerals. A message flashed: "CODE SYSTEM ALTERED." The alarm assaulted her ears as the numbers continued to whirl, until finally the message "AUTODESTRUCT" filled the display.

In her peripheral vision she saw movement on the

aboveground monitor, and turned to watch, fascinated. The video screen received a feed from a periscopelike camera mounted on the runway surface, and she gazed in wonder as a six-foot-high silver cylinder with a rounded top rose out of the concrete. The radio transmitter glinted menacingly in the sun. She didn't bother to stifle an involuntary laugh. It was perfect. Everything was in place. It would be virtually impossible for them to stop her, now that she'd got this far.

Inside the glass bubble, weather patterns fizzed and growled like caged beasts as the alarm whined its warning. She was momentarily distracted from the sight as uniformed guards raced into the control room, having passed the last air lock. She gathered herself and looked down on the guards. They would never know what had hit them, these little boys playing soldiers.

She leaped off the steel gantry, landing atop four of them, delivering four of her best lethal karate blows to each neck in its turn. They were dead by the time she scrambled to her feet, she knew. The others weren't near enough to stop her—even if they could, she thought—and she knew they would have orders not to shoot. Besides, they'd known her for years, trusted her. Her fellow Englishmen were so very civilized; it worked nicely to her advantage.

She raced away round the corner—only to find a phalanx of guards in attack formation, their truncheons raised. Preternaturally cool as she was, the sheer numbers of them gave her pause.

"Stop!" yelled the guard in front of her as she checked her speed. She wheeled, and the guard hesitated for one fatal instant. In that moment, she swiveled, somersaulted, and—with nearly superhuman grace and speed, if she did say so herself—double-kicked two guards, who fell limply to the ground.

She pivoted round, auburn hair whirling in a red tornado, as two more guards approached. With another spectacular double scissor-kick finish, she knocked them to the floor. She didn't pause, but sprang into the air again, defying gravity in an acrobatic flip that took her six feet into the air. She landed like a cat, bang in front of the exit door.

"Autodestruct countdown," came the voice over the intercom. "Evacuate! Repeat, evacuate! Autodestruct in ten . . . nine . . ." The remaining dozen or so guards ran for their lives toward the back of the room to the emergency escape tunnels. She knew about the tunnels, too, but she would use the main exit, the telephone booth near her car. The guards had been informed, she knew, that should autodestruct ever occur, they had precisely ten seconds to get out through the escape hatches. Pity she couldn't kill them all—how she longed to—but she'd have to let them go. Perhaps another day.

One conscientious guard—she recognized him as Derek Miller—turned back and raised his weapon at her, his eyes tortured. But he was too late. She ducked out the doorway and ran her fastest—not an inconsequential speed—to the vestibule leading to the phone box lift.

As she stood poised on her buckle-and-strap-laden leather boots, cool as dry ice, she heard the telltale whir of a camera. Perfect, she thought, and turned her face full to the lens. They've got their photo of Emma Peel destroying the Prospero lab. She was really rather proud of her work.

Reeling off the exit passwords, she said, "Doctor Foster went to Glo'ster in a shower of rain." The essential pause. "Saint Swithin's Day, if thou dost rain, for forty days it will remain." Her eyes gleamed eerily as the lift groaned to a start and carried her up to the airstrip.

A jolly good show, she thought, stepping smartly to her Jaguar. One to make even herself proud. Settling into her leather bucket seat, she looked back at her handiwork. A swirling black cloud full of electricity was floating menacingly toward the transmitter attached to the glass bubble. Full of crackling, electric energy, the twister hissed and buzzed as she watched, surging with power, discharging, then building again. A lightning bolt, thick and jagged, hit the silver transmitter. The next bolt made a direct hit, contradicting the old law that lightning never strikes twice.

This was no ordinary lightning storm. In fact, it was most unnatural. Below ground, inside the bizarre glass bubble, those were *man-made* weather systems fizzing and crackling like ticking bombs. And that's precisely what they were. Ticking bombs.

Suddenly she heard the glass of the great bubble splitting, saw the metal of the transmitter melting and running into its center—like mercury in a thermometer indicating a very sick patient indeed.

The few unfortunate guards and scientists remaining in the facility, she knew, would feel an odd sensation of pressure, as if they were developing a raging headache . . . and then they would feel no more. The forces inside the glass bubble would explode in a chemical-electric frenzy, destroying the control room and everyone in it with all the efficiency of a nuclear bomb. People, electronics, steel walls—all vaporized.

Barely able to suppress her excitement, she shifted into first and floored the accelerator. As the car raced along the airstrip, she adjusted her rearview mirror to better view the devastation as concrete rolled and then flew into the air behind her. She laughed wickedly at the disaster she had wrought. In the mirror, she watched the explosion ripple skyward, felt the shock waves of energy blast her in the car. At the edge of the airstrip she screeched to a halt, got out of the Jaguar and climbed atop it. There she stood, legs spread wide. She was breathing hard, arms wrapped around herself in ecstasy, feeling the dangerous acceleration of her heart. As if to make her climax complete, a lovely specimen of a mushroom cloud furled up into the sky before her.

She closed her eyes; her lips parted. She savored the moment, willing it to linger. She stood atop the Jaguar, hearing the roar of the explosion's aftermath, feeling the heat from the flames, and vibrations—possibly from some secondary blast. Shaking uncontrollably, she opened her eyes again. That was one to remember.

Very satisfying indeed.

CHAPTER TWO

. . . he did believe he was indeed the Duke . . . and executing th' outward face of royalty with all prerogative. Hence, his ambition growing . . .

The Tempest, *William Shakespeare*

When Farthing, the butler, peered in at the door to the library, he saw that his fears were justified. The master was having another episode. Of course, they'd become almost chronic now. Crashing chords of majestic organ music boomed into the vaulted cathedral ceiling of the room.

Farthing's view passed down the narrow aisle of the library. It was flanked by floor-to-ceiling books, lit with unearthly-colored sunshine streaming from lead stained glass windows. One would have been forgiven for mistaking it for a church, Farthing thought, except for the antique book of *Magus's Spells* and an unusual collection of rare meteorological tomes splayed wildly on a long oak trestle table.

His gaze passed still further through the library, un-

der an ornate, narrow archway, where at last he saw the
master. Sir August de Wynter was seated at the vast pipe
organ, which filled a smallish room of its own, pipes of
varying lengths covering the entire surface of one wall.
His hands moved wildly—brilliantly—over the keys, his
legs pumping furiously at the pedals all the while.

The organ seemed ready to explode with passion,
power, and magnificence, Farthing thought. He watched
with some fascination. Rocking and swaying, the master
seemed entranced by his own passionate playing. His
fingers accelerated in virtuoso arpeggios, until at last he
slammed the keyboard in a tingling vibrato . . . only to
culminate it all with a final, crashing chord. The sound,
Farthing thought with no small resentment, was positively deafening.

Peering round the door frame, he saw Sir August suddenly stand and turn away from the organ, applauding
himself. Horrified that he would be discovered, Farthing
withdrew slightly round the corner. The last chord continued to echo in the cathedral-like ceiling as Farthing
shook his head. It was a pity the master was so deranged. He really was a highly intelligent, talented, even
tasteful man.

Farthing ventured another peek round the door frame.
Sir August really was extremely handsome in his gray-
haired maturity. He had the body of a man half his
age, and piercing eyes like ice-blue laser beams. The
Queen had made him a Knight of the British Empire, and Farthing knew that at one time he'd headed
some supersecret scientific installation, right here in
Cambridgeshire. Yes, the master was brilliant, privi-
leged and accomplished. If it weren't for his bizarre
obsessions . . .

In his thirty years of service to the de Wynters, Farthing had witnessed some very strange spectacles. But
these last three years had really taken the biscuit. Bizarre

weather that existed nowhere else in the kingdom plagued
Hallucinogen Hall, the ancestral home of the de Wynters. More than once he'd driven through blizzardlike
conditions down the Hall's drive only to find peaceful
blue sky and fluffy white clouds at the main road.

And now the strange creature who'd suddenly appeared from nowhere, who looked like a woman, ate
like an animal, and spoke like a child. And the torture
chamber in the mirrored ballroom, with head clamps
and straps to restrain . . . whom? Not to mention the
vials of chemicals, marked "Poison" and decorated with
skull and crossbones, that arrived in carefully insulated
boxes.

He shook his head. It was not for him to judge. The
de Wynters had always been more than kind to him. But
he'd never expected Sir August to go quite this far down
the garden path.

Retreating further from the door, Farthing saw the
master gaze upward, heard him howl breathlessly.
"Bravo! Let our revels begin."

Farthing pursed his lips, rolled his eyes. Really, this
was most distasteful. He knew to whom the master was
speaking, and where he was looking. It was that portrait
of the beautiful Mrs. Emma Peel, who looked remark-
ably like the woman who'd come to live at the Hall.
Though from Sir August's conversation with the girl,
who didn't seem to have a name, she was clearly *not*
Emma Peel. Shaking his head again sadly he stepped
away from the door and walked with all due speed
toward the kitchen. This obsession of the master's could
only lead to tragedy. Sir August had worshipped the
woman for fifteen years, and it all seemed to be coming
to a head now.

Farthing hurried down the corridor, doing his best to
keep his shoes quiet against the wood floor. It wouldn't
do to be caught in the hallway by the master; no, it

wouldn't do at all. For the master was howling, *barking* mad. Many of the other, newer servants had simply disappeared.

Farthing shuddered. There was no telling what Sir August de Wynter might do.

CHAPTER THREE

What foul play had we that we came from thence?
Or blessèd was't we did?

The Tempest, *William Shakespeare*

The primly upturned brim of a black bowler hat was
the first thing to emerge from the village cake shop.
The shop bell jangled as John Steed, ducking his
head to avoid the doorjamb, stepped briskly out the
door. He turned to inspect the shop window; he'd
found that reflections in picture windows were always
useful in surveillance.

But all he saw were Bakewell tarts, buns, scones and a
year-old wedding cake—aside from his own reflection.
Bowler, old school tie, waistcoat, Savile Row suit jacket,
perfect trouser crease, umbrella hanging from his arm—
yes, all was in order. A final glance downward at his be-
spoke shoes determined that they did indeed reflect the
splendor of it all with mirrorlike shine.

The bells of the village church rang out the first phrase
of "Jerusalem," then chimed ten bells. Steed's reflection

faithfully reproduced the casual reach into his waistcoat pocket for his fob watch, showed laughing eyes flicking down to the watch and back.

Replacing the watch on its chain in his waistcoat, he adjusted his bowler and turned from the shop window to survey the narrow village street. It was the quintessential English village high street, cobbled, just wide enough for a horse and a carriage to negotiate between the shops. Aside from the baker, he saw signs for a pub, an auto repair garage, the newsagent's, and a fruiterer. The parish church was on the village common, a bit further down.

"Absolutely lovely day," Steed pronounced, quite enjoying the sound of his own voice. All too few children were trained to produce the mellifluous tones that had been natural to him from birth. Pronunciation, diction, timbre, elocution, resonance—these were a dying art in England. The abandonment of tradition could lead only to disaster, he reflected, sighing.

Steed heard an odd noise from overhead. Cocking his head curiously, he took one step to the side with studied nonchalance as a china vase smashed next to him in the street. Sharp shards of the stuff littered the cobbles, along with half a dozen red and white carnations. Steed kept his face inscrutable—his specialty—as he stepped back to study the window above, presumably the baker's flat. Nothing—except for white lace curtains waving mysteriously in the still morning.

"Hmm." Still expressionless, he stooped to pick up a red carnation and deftly slid the stem through his buttonhole.

Steed strolled into the lane, greeting the village policeman as he emerged from the pub. "Morning, constable," he said pleasantly.

The constable nodded a polite greeting, but once he'd passed Steed, he wheeled—hand poised to deliver a deadly karate chop. Steed heard the man's boot begin to turn on the cobbles, the whoosh of his clothing as he raised his arm, and swung round himself. Steed parried and thrust—so convenient to have a black belt, he thought—until the policeman fell, writhing on the ground.

Steed doffed his hat momentarily in deference to the fallen officer, brushed a speck of dust off his jacket, and strolled on. The village dairy's milk float rolled toward him innocuously, its electric motor whirring. Steed nodded pleasantly to the milkman, who stood, hefted two empty pint bottles and broke them against the float. Jumping down onto the street, he brandished the jagged remainders of the bottles in Steed's face. Perhaps this milkman had been threatened by one too many snarling dogs, Steed thought. Bit of a temper . . . or distemper . . .

The milkman lunged. With lightning speed, Steed thrust his umbrella out in front of him with both hands as if it were a vaudeville actor's cane. He whisked it upward under the man's arms, with enough force that the unfortunate fellow tumbled backward onto the cobbles, hitting his head on the stones with a *clunk* that made Steed wince. The jagged bottles flew into the air; Steed watched with satisfaction as they rained down on his attacker.

Steed straightened his coat and walked on, touching the brim of his hat to an elderly woman in sensible shoes pushing a pram. She smiled sweetly at him, nodding in acknowledgment. "Lovely day," he began, then saw that she had slipped a bundle of knives out from under the baby's bunting. Their blades glinted as she threw them expertly in his direction. Ducking, he heard them whistle past and plant themselves harmlessly in a garage mechanic's door on the other side of the narrow road.

As if on cue, two burly mechanics thundered out of the garage door bearing heavy chains, coming straight for him. Again, Steed countered skillfully with his brolly, but this time he pulled off the furled fabric exterior of the instrument to reveal a sword. He fought off their clumsy lengths of chain effortlessly with his weapon of choice, enjoying their expressions as his single fine piece of metal dominated over their larger, heavier ones. When he'd tired of the game, one at a time, while they were attempting to hoist the heavy links up for another round, he gave each of them just enough of a poke in their ample midsections to send them reeling to the ground.

As they lay groaning and clutching their bellies, worrying they had been mortally wounded, Steed said, "Sorry," shot his cuffs and continued down the high street. Bit of an unfriendly place, this, he thought, frowning. Almost enough to make one feel unwelcome. At that moment, three nuns crossed his path, their black habits sweeping the cobbles.

"Morning. Splendid day for a stroll," he said to the nuns, smiling as they disappeared into the pub. He was musing on the modern attitudes of these brides of Christ when he glimpsed a shadow. He looked up as a car skidded round the corner at top speed, right at him.

Hmm. *Bit of a sticky wicket,* Steed thought. There was nowhere at all to hide on the narrow street, and there was no time . . . With effortless grace, if he did say so himself, Steed reached his umbrella up. He held it this time by the steel tip and hooked the rosewood handle over the pub sign, hoisting himself up as the car zoomed directly beneath his shiny oxfords. The car screeched to a stop just inches away.

While Steed hung from his umbrella as if it were the most natural thing on earth, a slouching, bookish man in a white coat emerged from the car. In his hand was a stopwatch.

"Well done, Steed," he said, nodding in admiration.

"My pleasure, Dr. Darling," said Steed, dropping
down. He straightened his lapels and picked up his umbrella, continuing down the street with Darling. They
turned the corner and emerged into an office area, filled
with desks and phones. A young bespectacled bureau-
crat in a white coat held up a clipboard bearing six large
numbers, written in heavy black marker, for Steed's bene-
fit. *Just like an ice-skating judge,* Steed thought, as he regarded the five tens and one nine.

Steed cocked his eyebrows at the man. "What's the
nine for, then?"

"A bit slow on the garage mechanics, I thought.
Otherwise, you'll do."

Steed nodded briskly and looked round the room.
The fake set that housed the laboratory assault course
was actually a rather pleasant little village; he'd enjoyed
his stroll. It was a shame it all had to dissolve into fax
machines and phones.

Reading his look, Dr. Darling offered, "You never
know . . ."

". . . When the enemy will strike. Yes. *If* we still have
an enemy. . . ."

Dr. Darling took up a rubber stamp from the desk
nearest them. With a flourish, he stamped "TOP SE-
CRET" on a thick document bearing both the royal in-
signia and the Ministry logo. The bright red capital
letters jumped out at Steed. He knew where Darling was
heading with this.

Looking grimly at Steed, Darling continued. "Always
an enemy, Steed. Just have to know where to look. . . ."
Ominously, he broke off, glancing briefly at the document. He blinked, then cast a furtive glance around
them before looking up again at Steed. "Something's up
at the Ministry. They want you to meet somebody."

"They know where to find me," Steed said, deposit-
ing a gold box wrapped in shiny red ribbons on the

desk. In answer to Darling's curious look, he said, "Macaroons. For Mother." He strode off, swinging his furled brolly, and exited into the great out-of-doors.

Looking up at some rather threatening-looking clouds, he said, with the ghost of a smile, "Rain on the way, I think."

CHAPTER FOUR

Hark what thou else shalt do me . . .
The Tempest, *William Shakespeare*

Steed was a vision on the streets of London, gliding down the road in his sleek green Bentley. He'd known no other car; this one had been in the family for . . . let's see . . . nearly forty years now. *Sweet tradition,* he thought. *And people say British motorcars are unreliable. Pish-tosh.*

He looked untroubled as, out of the open top, the car radio announcer's voice said urgently, "An explosion devastated the countryside in Cambridgeshire, near a science research establishment . . ."

At that moment the Bentley backfired repeatedly. Steed was forced to acknowledge the one drawback of driving a car steeped in tradition. Pedestrians cringed at the noise, which sounded exactly like a round from a loaded pistol. The news announcer continued, competing with the noise of the backfiring vehicle. Steed turned up the radio volume. "Meanwhile, the War Office confirmed that the historic meeting of the World Council of Ministers will herald a new global defense treaty. . . ."

Steed drove on, heading toward Chelsea. A woman he'd heard about for quite some time lived there, a Dr. Emma Peel, and he wanted to conduct a quiet little reconnaissance of her neighborhood. He was to work with her—or, rather, to let her *think* they were working together. His job was actually to kill her, because she had blown up one of the nation's most vital research establishments—her own place of employment for a good many years. One never knew why treasonous traitors committed their crimes.

But Steed wondered if perhaps he might not strike a little defense treaty of his own with her . . . the photos Dr. Darling had shown him were really quite striking. And for years every eligible male—and ineligible male, as well—had been agog over her. Word was that her superior intelligence was only excelled by her physical prowess. Steed had never met her himself, but his luck was about to change.

If Dr. Darling knew what he was about, things were hotting up indeed. He sighed. These secret assignments could be so taxing . . . perhaps he'd spend a bit of time relaxing at the club before meeting Mrs. Peel. Ah, yes. And the club was the perfect place for another sort of reconnaissance. . . .

Emma Peel was fast asleep in bed when her buzzer rang. She opened her eyes, realized that it was indeed her doorbell making that dreadful racket, and groaned. Relishing the comfort of her pillow, she gave it another moment before throwing off the bedclothes and sitting on the edge of the bed.

Dr. Peel was not unaccustomed to such calls. As she sat yawning, she reflected that the one thing she'd learned in this business was to always be prepared. No one would believe the things she'd seen in her twenty-eight years, and she wasn't allowed to tell them, anyway. Part of always being prepared, like a good Girl Guide, was always being dressed. She hadn't slept in nightclothes for nearly a decade.

She stood, stretching, wearing a smooth black sheath dress of stretchy knit. The muscles in her calves rippled as she slipped into the stiletto heels by her bedroom door. Then she stepped onto the metal bridge that cut across the two levels of her flat and led to the stairway to the ground floor. As she crossed the vast white open space, she surveyed her surroundings with satisfaction. Three separate Chelsea houses had sat on this spot before she'd knocked them all together into one. Heaven knew, it wouldn't do to have anything traditional. The country was going under with the weight of it all.

She strode down the stairs in her steel-heeled shoes past abstract modern paintings, enjoying her usual thrill of proprietary pleasure. Below, on the main level, were several seating areas consisting of pastel candy-colored chairs and glass tables.

At the door, Emma flicked open the automated eye, peering through at an innocent-looking messenger in a uniform. She unfastened all six deadbolt locks and swung open the door. She eyed the young man intently as he inquired, "Dr. Peel?" and handed over a gold box tied with a red bow.

"Thank you." She shut the door and untied the bow, then lifted off the lid of the box. An embossed card rested on top. Emma read it aloud. "Please answer the telephone."

She looked at her phone, which was absolutely silent, and shrugged. But as she turned away again, it began to ring. She picked up and heard a recorded message, which sounded as if it had been made by the speaking-clock woman of days gone by: "Boodle's Club, two-thirty P.M.

Mr. John Steed . . . Boodle's Club, two-thirty P.M. Mr. John Steed . . ." The phone beeped once and went dead. Emma looked at the box in her hand; unfolded the tissue from the top. Choccies. Puzzled, she popped one into her mouth.

"Ah. Rum truffle. Whoever this Steed is, he has good taste."

Emma pulled her powder-blue Jaguar E-type into the last parking space in front of the white stucco buildings in Pall Mall that housed Boodle's Club. She climbed out, to the appreciative stares of passersby, in a white leather ensemble that left little to the imagination: a miniskirt, bustier, and jacket. Her knee-high high-heeled white leather boots and a long, diaphanous turquoise scarf set it all off, but she neither acknowledged the looks she received nor seemed to enjoy them. For Emma Peel dressed only to please herself . . . and for the rigors of her work.

As she walked coolly toward the Boodle's entrance, she passed the black-on-white sign of a news vendor: "MYSTERIOUS EXPLOSION: DEFENCE ALERT."

Mounting the steps to the club, she noted the inscription on the brass plaque at the door: "Boodle's Gentleman's Club." She opened the door and stepped in, past an astonished uniformed commissionaire.

Inside the clubby reception area, a fiftyish porter approached her, stunned that she dared to darken his hallowed doorway. "May I help you, madam?" His mouth turned down at the corners, a souvenir, Emma thought, from decades of snobbery and disapproval.

Emma smiled pleasantly. "For Mr. John Steed. I'm Dr. Peel."

The porter looked away from her and indulged himself in a condescending sneer of a smile. "Oh, dear," he said sarcastically. "I'm afraid that madam is much mistaken. It's simply not possible, you see."

He pointed to a notice that read, in deliberately offensive fashion, thought Emma: "NO NON-MEMBERS. NO ANIMALS. NO WOMEN."

The porter squinted at her white leather resplendence, his eyes widening briefly. "You *are* female?" The corners of his mouth twitched in wry amusement.

Emma leaned close, so that he couldn't help but get a glimpse of what was visible at the top of the bustier. "As you see."

It was too much, even for His Frostiness. Blushing, the porter blinked and looked away. "You . . . I'm sorry . . . then you can't come in."

"I have an appointment," Emma declared pleasantly.

He closed his eyes for a moment in exasperation. When he opened them again, he refused to look at her. "No women. Not in Boodle's. Not since 1783."

"Oh, really?" Emma asked, feigning interest. "What happened in 1783?"

The porter was busy opening his mouth to speak when Emma breezed by, cool as the proverbial cucumber, and stepped into the hall. She was instantly surrounded by a cocoon of old mahogany and leather chairs. Well, she'd been inside male enclaves like this before. If they only knew . . .

The porter lunged at her from behind, but, half expecting such folly, she sidestepped him with a delicate jujitsu move. She selected a book from a shelf and checked its copyright page for a first edition as he tumbled straight past her, down a flight of stairs opposite. On and on he tumbled, head over heels. To his credit, he didn't cry out as the steps pummeled his soft, fleshy body. At last the grunting and thumping stopped, and the stifled groans began.

That was that, then. Closing the book and sliding it

back onto the shelf, she peered down the stairway and said, "Thank you so much. I can find Mr. Steed myself."

The man stared up at her in a daze.

Emma strolled on, toward a set of massive double doors. She gazed at her surroundings, and was interested to see a pair of naked bronze warriors frowning down on her from the balcony above. So that was how the men of Boodle's wished to see themselves. She hated to be the one to tell them, but from what she'd seen so far . . .

She gave the warriors a small salute, frowning back at them, then pushed through the doors and found herself in what was clearly the library. Elegant bookcases lined the walls from floor to ceiling, and Emma strutted matter-of-factly through chairs and tables filled with old men drinking and smoking—very few actually reading, she noted.

Giving them the once-over she saw, as she had suspected, that they were going to have to do a good bit of dieting and bodybuilding to look anything like the bronze warriors to which they aspired. The members' fusty old relics collected dust on the tables next to them; humidors, pipes, sculptures of men on horses, useless paperweights, antique globes, inkwells. Even the air felt several centuries old, and smelled of mustiness run amok. As she *tick-tack*ed past in her steel-heeled boots, one of the elderly members gasped audibly. Newspapers crinkled. Books slapped shut, and one fell to the floor. The entire room gaped.

"Good afternoon, gentlemen," she said coolly, and continued on through the room to another set of double doors. She rather liked hearing the sound of her own voice. All too few Britons these days spoke with proper pronunciation, diction, timbre, elocution, resonance. . . .

Pushing through the doors, she saw a sign that read, "Oriental Room." Steam seeped out the cracks round the door. "Hmm," she said, and pulled it open. A cloud of steam engulfed her, but she thought she perceived a man sitting naked, save for a towel in the critical spot. He had a bowler hat at his side, of all things, and appeared to be reading a very soggy peach-colored newspaper. She heard him mumble, "Rain tomorrow, then. Hmm. Right under this 'Mysterious explosion' article . . ."

Emma eyed him as he read, talking to himself. She'd read somewhere that this strange, self-indulgent habit was the hallmark of genius. And she noted with interest that he didn't have so very far to go in his quest to resemble the bronze warriors. Yes—not half-bad. He even read her favorite newspaper, the *Financial Times*.

Suddenly he seemed to perceive Emma through the mist, turning his head in her direction. "Doctor Peel, I presume?"

"And you must be Steed. Please—don't get up," she added. She didn't want *that* much of him revealed to her at once. She saw the twinkle in his eye that showed he caught her meaning. *Good,* she thought. But what did he want?

They studied each other, the only sound the steam hissing between them. Emma remained standing near the door.

"I was about to throw in the towel," Steed confessed, lowering his paper.

"Sorry. A spot of bother at the door."

"I shouldn't wonder," he said with some enthusiasm. "Not a woman inside Boodle's since—"

"Seventeen-eighty-three. Until you invited me here." Crossing her arms in front of her, she looked around the white marble-clad room, evaluating. "So what was all this—some sort of test?"

"Mmm. Congratulations. You've entered a bastion of male privilege. You aren't someone who plays by the rules, Doctor." She thought she saw a smile at one end of his mouth, but wasn't sure. He had a lovely speaking voice.

"Rules are made to be broken."

"Not by me. Play by the rules, Doctor. Or the game is nothing." He studied her, allowing the hiss of the steam to emphasize his statement.

"And just what *is* the game?" Emma asked, amused.

"I say, this is all terribly formal. Must I go on calling you Dr. Peel?"

She paused for thought. "Mmm. Under the circumstances, you may call me Mrs. Peel."

"Much better."

"Now that we've settled the matter of titles, will you kindly explain why you wished to meet me?"

"*I* didn't," said the man in the towel. "Mother did."

"Mother?"

"Mother."

Steed finished toweling dry in the locker room. Mrs. Peel had got a bit hot in the steam room, and would be waiting for him outside the club's rear door. His colleague's reports had been far from accurate. She was stunning. Really. And a lovely voice, as well. A bit untraditional in the clothing department, but he could live with that.

He brought out pieces of clothing one at a time, as needed, from his mahogany-fronted cupboard. Dressing was a fine art, not to be rushed or taken lightly. If he didn't maintain the standard, who knew what disaster might result? Certainly the next generation would have no example to follow. Besides, the prime minister sometimes came to the Ministry, and to Boodle's, for that matter, to pay a visit. It wouldn't do to be sloppily attired.

Dr. Emma Peel . . . Mrs. Emma Peel. Pulling on his trousers, Steed found it hard to believe that she could be responsible for the Prospero disaster. Though her eyes teased, he considered himself a good judge of character, and he'd had the distinct feeling from the moment he'd laid eyes on her that she was a good egg. Besides the teasing, her eyes betrayed enough intelligence to convince him that she wouldn't stoop to sabotage or terrorism.

No, Steed thought, there was a greater mystery there. As he buttoned his shirt, he knew he would have to help her find out who *had* blown up the secret laboratory, else her career would be over.

More than that, he would never see her again, because she'd be put away for good. And that simply wouldn't do. Steed flipped a switch at the back of his locker, then peered into the lighted mirror inside and tied his tie. As he pulled the brightly colored old school stripes through a loop at his neck, he eyed himself critically. Would she find him attractive?

Judging from her reaction in the steam room, she hadn't exactly been repulsed. But she was not to be underestimated, Steed knew. After carefully brushing his hair, he swung the locker door closed and turned the key in the lock, then pocketed it. Strange, really; Mrs. Emma Peel was the first woman for whom he'd felt respect, admiration, and lust in equal proportions.

It was a new sensation, and therefore suspect.

Steed's green Bentley zoomed down the Embankment as Big Ben chimed the hour. Emma rode in the passenger seat; Steed drove. Neither spoke until Steed said, "Four o'clock. Mustn't be late."

"Time for tea?"

"Yes. A word of warning. Don't take the macaroon. Mother's favorite."

Emma acted as if this were perfectly plausible and made no comment as Steed swerved into the secret car park entrance by the riverbank. The car came to a stop before a sign that read: "THAMES RIVER AUTHORITY.

NO ADMITTANCE." At the control barrier, Steed inserted a thin plastic card. A red light flashed as a small display blinked the words, "Security—Top Priority Clearance Only."

The barrier lifted as Emma looked at Steed, reappraising him. Big Ben continued to chime, as if marking a solemn occasion. As the car disappeared into the darkness of the subterranean car park, she thought perhaps tea today might be rather more interesting than usual.

CHAPTER FIVE

Thou liest, malignant thing!
The Tempest, *William Shakespeare*

A film projector flickered images into the darkness as Emma watched. She had been seated next to Steed, and Mother next to him. Mother, it turned out, was an odd-looking gent confined to a wheelchair—a man Emma wouldn't have trusted if this hadn't been the Ministry. His sinister appearance was aided by dark, slicked-back hair that made him look positively gangster-like, Emma thought. But she'd had bigger surprises, such as the fact that the Ministry's offices were entirely underwater, beneath the River Thames.

Emma redirected her attention to the scratchy, snowy, black-and-white film footage. Bizarre, distressing images passed before her eyes: cows on parched grass, lawn bowls in a snowdrift, horses standing knee-deep in water.

The man called Mother said, "First it was the Chew

Lakes evaporating, then Kent pastureland turning overnight into African scrub. A whole series of bizarre weather reports . . ."

Emma and Steed looked at Mother at the same time, noticed that they had done so, and glanced at each other. Steed raised his eyebrows at her ever so slightly. *Good Lord,* Emma thought. The last time anyone had thought the same thing at the same time as she had been . . .

Despair washed over her as she pulled her eyes away from Steed's. She told herself for the millionth time to stop thinking about her husband. He was dead. There was no bringing him back now. And no one would ever be as suitable for her as he had been. It was as if the two of them had been made for . . .

Emma pulled herself back into the present with an effort as Mother continued. "One Surrey village recorded victims of sunburn and frostbite on the same day," he intoned, sounding grim. "Freak temperatures of one hundred and fifty degrees."

"Well?" said Emma, unimpressed.

Sounding a bit exasperated, Mother's voice rose. "On the hottest day of the year, half its football team froze to death."

"Time to get your woolens," Emma said breezily.

"The weather's turning nasty," Mother said with clenched teeth, his glare reprimanding her for such flippancy.

Emma frowned in the darkness. She'd heard about the odd weather long ago. There'd been reports of such occurrences round the world over the past few years. In fact, there always *had* been fluky weather, and there always *would* be. Some people saw a conspiracy in everything. When her voice came, it sounded bored. "There's no discernible pattern here. We had an expert system tracking all these reports at the lab."

Quietly, Mother said, "We went further. Sent our

best scientists into the field. Most are missing . . . or dead."

Illustrating his point most graphically, the screen displayed a series of macabre scenes of death. One man had been trapped in ice, another had spontaneously combusted. Still another lay dead in a dry riverbed of equally dead fish.

"Ah," she said. "I see." When there were fallen agents to justify, weather suddenly became important to the Ministry. Well, surely they couldn't expect her to create a conspiracy for them.

In fact, why was *she* the one involved here? They didn't need her doctorate in meteorological sciences to tell them there was bizarre weather in the world. A pity their scientists had blundered into it. For that matter, where were the other Prospero scientists? Why hadn't they gone to the head of the entire program, to Professor Quick?

Something odd was afoot, and had been from the rum truffles onward. Emma felt the skin prickle at the back of her neck.

Steed knew that Mrs. Peel's reactions were being monitored on the secret video screen behind the wall. He wondered how her performance was being evaluated. He also wondered exactly who she really was. Was she a long-trusted government scientist? Or *was* she a treasonous saboteur? Either way, she was damned attractive. And the more he thought about it, the white leather clothing suited her. She simply wasn't at all like other women; so why dress like them?

Mother continued. "Frankly, we're baffled. The weather's changing. Fast. We want to know why."

"Global warming?" Steed piped up. "Or man-made?"

"That about covers it," Emma said. Steed again noticed the musical quality of her speaking voice. Not unlike his own . . . but female. And tastefully pitched at the lower end of the scale. Most unusual.

"Exactly," Mother said, wheeling himself in front of the screen. The beam illuminated his decidedly unattractive features, including bulbous nose and slick hair, as the devastation of the Prospero weather station played on the screen and double-exposed on his face. "The Prospero Program."

Mother brought up the lights and pulled on a cord. The wooden blinds lifted to reveal a wall of water. Steed, glancing at Mrs. Peel, saw that she almost raised her eyebrows. Wheeling himself round, Mother said, "I always prefer a room with a view, don't you?" He picked up the teapot. "Tea? I'll be mother. . . ."

Mother fulfilled his promise, pouring, and Steed saw Emma glance round the bizarre headquarters of their elite intelligence force. Wooden duckboards covered leaky areas in the underwater HQ, and oppressive humidity lent the ambiance of a locker room. Steed could almost see her thinking that if those leaky walls gave way, they weren't likely to survive for a swim to the top. Mother would be at a decided disadvantage.

"I know about the Prospero Program explosion," Emma said calmly. "Sugar, please. One lump . . . Is that why I'm here?"

Mother looked up and met her eyes as he placed the lump in her tea with great delicacy, using small silver tongs, as if it were a cube of poison. "You're here for tea, Dr. Peel." His voice was utterly noncommittal.

A woman's voice came from behind Mother, out of the darkness. "Welcome to the Ministry. Macaroon?" The voice belonged to a young woman, clad in a crisp blue suit with short dark hair framing bright eyes. She wheeled a cake trolley out of nowhere.

Steed knew that this was Brenda, Mother's miniskirted bodyguard and executive assistant. Mother hadn't done too badly there, he thought. Brenda winked at Steed

as she passed with the trolley. It was most unfair the way
he led her on, Steed told himself. Must do something
about that someday. But in the meantime, Brenda was
quite useful to him. As she'd said so often, she'd do anything . . . anything at all. . . .

Steed saw Emma squint suspiciously at Brenda, perceiving the offer of a macaroon as a trick. Steed had
warned her about the macaroons.

Frowning, Steed saw that there might be a bit of jeal-
ousy on Brenda's part. She knew all too well what
would happen if Mrs. Peel took Mother's favorite biscuits. Yes, she might be trying to turn the tide against
Mrs. Peel.

Steed deftly changed the subject. Such a useful skill in
these minor emergencies. "Prospero . . . very Shakespearean. Do explain."

"Top-secret research," Emma replied. "A government
project I was working on to create a weather shield."
She looked directly at Steed, then at the umbrella by his
side, and translated for him. "A defensive umbrella, if
you will, Mr. Steed."

He was grateful for this small courtesy. "Ah! I see.
Someone attacks . . . we put up this umbrella . . . everyone goes home for tea. Marvelous."

"Until someone blows up the research lab." Emma
sipped at her tea, apparently unconcerned.

"Did they just walk in?" Steed asked. "How did they
get past security?"

"That's what's interesting," Mother said gravely. "Security cameras at the Prospero lab picked up a picture
during the attack." Here he handed Emma a photo of
herself. "Recognize her, Mrs. Peel?"

Mrs. Peel stared. Steed noted with fascination that
the normally inscrutable woman's mouth actually fell
open. Eyes wide, her attention rapt, Mrs. Peel murmured, "Like a twin sister . . ."

"I say," Steed exclaimed. "She *does* look terribly familiar."

Steed knew that behind the walls, the analysts were probably zooming in with closeups on the hidden video screens, dissecting her every expression, counting her eye movements, analyzing her voice. Lucky fellows.

"This is a special assignment, Dr. Peel. With a twist." Mother paused for effect. "You're our chief suspect."

"I'm innocent . . . of course," Mrs. Peel said, having recovered her composure.

"Or," Steed said, pausing to select a chocolate-covered shortbread finger from the cake plate, "guilty until proven innocent."

"Why would I sabotage my own project?" Mrs. Peel asked.

"You tell us," Mother said coldly.

Mrs. Peel frowned and took a bite of Garibaldi biscuit. She chewed, regarding the photo on the table. "She looks like me. But she isn't."

Steed looked back to Mother, who pressed a button on an audio tape player on the table. Mother spoke, sounding grim, as the tape began to play. "We received this communiqué . . . anonymous, of course."

A male voice Emma didn't recognize drifted out over the room from the tape player. "Act One begins with a tempest, one of Prospero's powers. A fine performance by Mrs. Peel. One the World Council of Ministers will soon admire. . . ."

Mother switched off the damning tape with a click.

Steed watched Emma's face as she absorbed the bad news. Most people would be at least slightly concerned, but her face was now impressively inscrutable, a sort of tabula rasa. Not unlike his own, actually. Perhaps they really did have a bit in common.

"Given your years of impeccable and loyal service, you'll be allowed a privilege," Mother said. "To prove your innocence."

Mrs. Peel turned her lips up into a cold little smile. "To be precise, you're saying I have no choice."

She was quick, too, Steed thought.

"The World Council of Ministers is meeting next week to sign a treaty. Here, in London. We don't have much time. Find out what's going on. And quickly . . ."

Steed turned to Mrs. Peel, gesturing as if to say, "Shall we?" She stood cooperatively, but plucked a macaroon off the tray before moving toward the door. She bit into it while looking into Mother's eyes. Steed saw him receive the challenge. At least this Mrs. Peel wasn't one to avoid a confrontation, Steed thought.

On the way to the door, he said civilly, "Mother wants me to show you the ropes. He'd like us to work as a team."

When they had stepped out of the Ministry office into the subterranean hallway and closed the door, Mrs. Peel stopped short. Hands on her hips, she threw him a canny look. "You mean, I *have* to trust you."

She knew exactly what they were up to, Steed realized. Steed was to be her baby-sitter, her jailer . . . if necessary, her killer. Yet also, somehow, he felt he might also be her advocate.

Steed nodded at her in cheerful acknowledgment of all this. No need to be unpleasant about things, he always said.

"Absolutely, Mrs. Peel. At your beck and call. Shall we?"

Emma glared at him, a deadly, hateful stare, as he escorted her down the hallway.

When the door had closed behind them, locking, Dr. Darling and a slim, tastefully dressed woman with oddly glassy eyes emerged from the secret room. Mother spoke. "Think she killed those scientists, Father?"

The elegant woman named Father wore an earpiece,

which she pulled out of her ear impatiently as she answered. Her dark hair had been elaborately coiffed in a complicated, twisted chignon. "All in my report, Mother." Her every word fell hard and cold on Mother's ears, like a succession of ice cubes into a glass. Her hard face might have been chiseled out of the same material, so cold was its expression.

"Why haven't I read it?"

"Because I haven't given it to you. My theory is that Dr. Peel may be ill. . . ."

Mother looked up from the walls of files, where he had begun to search for something. "Really. Amnesia? Hypnosis?"

"Possibly," Father answered, frost in her voice. Mother perceived that Father was not overly smitten with Dr. Peel. "Split personality," she continued, "maybe trauma. There was a husband. . . ."

She paused, as if gauging Mother's reaction to this. "Test pilot, missing over the Amazon. Presumed dead. He was one of ours."

Mother sighed. "What a loss." He thought for a moment. "Revenge is a possible motive, then."

"She certainly fits our profile."

"Mrs. Peel's our only lead," Mother said with resignation. "Either she'll lead us to the real enemy, or they'll find her."

"She knows too much," Father said. "May be a risk. Admit it, Mother. If she is, there's only one solution. . . ." She turned to face Mother directly. "Termination."

CHAPTER SIX

*My affections are then most humble; I have no
ambition to see a goodlier man.*

The Tempest, *William Shakespeare*

Brenda picked up the tea things carefully, deep in
thought. Mother and Father had just had a bit of a
showdown. It had been lovely to see John again;
heaven knew he didn't come in out of the field often
enough.

She didn't mind this sort of work at all, she thought,
stacking the used plates. All she had to do was remind
herself of John Steed, and what a noble public servant
he was . . . risking his life night and day for the people
of England . . . just thinking about his selflessness could
make her cry.

She swiped away a tear and picked up the plate of
crumbs that had been his, cradling it reverently in both
hands. Inspecting the crumbs, she saw he'd had shortbread, something chocolaty, and cake. Good. He was

staying well fed. She placed his plate on the trolley carefully, and moved on to the cups.

Brenda frowned. She had her doubts about this Mrs. Peel. It rather sounded as if she belonged to the other side . . . but John would be clever enough to suss that out.

Brenda began humming "Rule, Britannia" as she placed the pot on the trolley and wheeled it toward the canteen.

Emma maintained inscrutability as Steed accelerated out of the top-secret car park. She hadn't wanted to let on, but she'd found Mother's photo of her in Prospero Program headquarters quite disturbing. There'd been an unfortunate episode in her career, shortly after her husband's death, when she'd been too slow to react in a fight with a Russian agent. He'd kicked her in the head, and when she'd come round she hadn't been able to remember certain things, among them her name, what she had done in the past, and where she'd been that day.

Very occasionally since then she'd worried about her memory. The steel-trap mind her university professors had raved about was precious to her, and it would be her second-greatest loss if it had been permanently damaged. She felt Steed glance at her, but didn't turn to meet his eyes. She stared instead at the lion statues in Trafalgar Square. A wonder someone hadn't pinched them, she thought. For the first time she noticed that their paws were outstretched, as if in anticipation of a giant kitty treat.

Or had she noticed that before and forgotten? She rested her chin on her hand, doing her best to camouflage her thoughts. What if she were a different person by night? What if she really *had* destroyed her own headquarters yesterday? She felt a tiny furrow forming between her eyebrows and relaxed the muscles. Mustn't let on to Steed, above all.

There was that month, after she'd heard about her husband's fiery death, that she hadn't been herself. She had traveled, in her mind, to dark places she had actively avoided ever since. What if those dark places hadn't disappeared, but had lurked in her subconscious mind until now—a hidden psychosis? For it *had* been she in that photo. There was no question about it.

In one of those frighteningly dark places she had successfully forgotten, she actually dreamt, while under sedation by a doctor, that the Prospero headquarters *had* exploded. That she had stood at the control dial and pumped antimatter into the test weather globe until it blew. She had interpreted the dream as meaning that her world had blown apart—a subconscious exploration of the idea that the explosion of her personal life might trigger one in her professional life.

Emma became aware that her fingers had clenched into a fist, and carefully relaxed them as Steed glanced over at her. His expression was as veiled as her own. Was it possible she had reverted to the dark place— without even knowing it—and had blown her lab and her colleagues into a million tiny bits?

It was unthinkable.

It was a distinct possibility.

The sign hanging outside Trubshaw's sport outfitter's in Jermyn Street was a large open umbrella, the name in gold fitted onto the massive brolly, with a pair of Wellington boots sheltering beneath it.

Inside, on the upper balcony, Steed and Emma were crossing fencing swords, testing out new blades—and each other. An elderly Trubshaw's employee carried on with paperwork behind the counter as if his customers parried with razor-sharp blades in the store every day.

"The Prospero Program was really very simple," Emma said, one hand on her hip as she expertly *tick-tack*ed her blade against Steed's. "We were bombarding protons and ions to make antimatter. . . ."

"I'd better start calling you 'doctor' again," Steed said. "Weight on the back foot, Mrs. Peel . . ."

Smiling, she let him believe that she accepted his advice on fencing technique.

Their blades crossed, *tick-tack, tick-tack*, six beats to the second, bringing her back to the present. Well, some things were simply better proved than said. *He's not bad,* Emma thought, *just needs challenging a bit.*

"We were artificially creating new weather systems," she continued.

"You're a lady of hidden talents, Mrs. Peel. . . . A little more flexibility in the wrist . . ."

There he goes again, she thought. She ignored the advice and wondered if one of her hidden talents—unbeknownst even to herself—was blowing up secret research facilities. During the day, normally, she worked as a mild-mannered meteorologist; but perhaps by night she was a psychopathic killer.

Tick-tack, tick-tack, tick-tack . . .

"Scientist . . . swordsperson . . . to what do you attribute your over-achievements?" Steed asked.

In a bit of fast swordplay, including a deft traditional *tac-au-tac* maneuver, Emma showed him her stuff. *He's not really that bad,* she thought grudgingly. *In fact, he'd handled that thrust rather well.*

Steed tossed her a look that said, *Touché.*

"My father always wanted a boy," Emma explained.

"Really? I fail to see the connection."

He was like the rest of his sex. "I had a feeling you would. So did he."

Emma lunged, and the foil tip pierced the heart on Steed's fencing costume.

At that moment, an impeccably attired elderly gentle-man stepped onto the balcony. "Bravo!" he said, blue eyes sparkling. Emma thought he looked as if perhaps he had been an athlete in his day. Something about the tight skin of his face . . . "May I have the honor . . . ?" He looked expectantly at Steed.

"Mr. Trubshaw, I give you Dr. Emma Peel, expert swordsperson."

"A pleasure." Trubshaw offered a small, gallant bow in her direction.

Steed swished his weapon upright and weighted it like a knight, then handed it over to Trubshaw. Emma handed him her blade, and Trubshaw passed them both to the assistant behind the counter. The old gentleman led the way to another display case, against the far wall, indicating that they should follow. He pressed a button, and a black velvet-lined shelf slid out from the wall, re-vealing a samurai-like display of umbrella handles at-tached to swords.

That's why Steed always carries an umbrella, Emma thought. *It's his little weapon. Wouldn't he be surprised to know where I carry mine. . . .*

She smiled at the thought as the two gentlemen leaned over the display.

"There's nothing like the strength of ebony," Trub-shaw was saying. "When I was in India . . ."

Steed said mildly, "The ebony handles are a touch heavy. I'll stick to the rosewood."

"The solid crook, sir?" Trubshaw inquired. Steed nodded.

Emma watched the entire formal exchange with fas-cination. This Steed was some specimen. Did he mean it all as a joke, she wondered?

"Excellent, sir," Trubshaw intoned. "If you'll walk this way . . ."

He led them down the steps. Downstairs, Trubshaw's

was a more conventional male outfitter's. Hunting trophies mounted on the walls watched as men tried on pink coats held by attendants in tails and wing-collars. Emma breezed through the male bastion flirtatiously, aware that every eye in the place was fixed on her.

She picked up a brown leather riding crop and slapped the tip of it against her palm with impatience. "Now my knight has chosen his armor, shouldn't we be on our way?"

Steed held up a hand, as if to say, not so fast. "Trubshaw's a man worth meeting. No point in setting out half-shod. That's why I've taken the liberty of ordering you a pair of boots, Mrs. Peel."

"Why, thank you." She thought for a moment, slapping the crop against her leg meditatively. So John Steed had a boot fetish. Perhaps he was a leather man. Did he always buy women leather boots, almost immediately after meeting them? For all she knew it could be his little habit. "If you'll pardon my asking, how did you know my size?"

Steed looked marginally uncomfortable. It was the first time she had seen him so. He cleared his throat and spoke quietly, watching the crop. "My . . . er . . . *employer* has extensive records."

Trubshaw spoke, as if to rescue his prize customer. Giving her a slightly wide-eyed once-over, he said, "Madam will appreciate our expertise in leather."

"Ah. Excellent. Well, thank you." Emma moved on to the tie display, fiddling with the bright stripes of silk on the glass counter. Trubshaw fussed with a new waistcoat he was fitting on Steed as Emma waited. Was the man going to go over Steed's entire wardrobe, piece by piece?

"Old school ties," she said, resigning herself to a long wait. "How quaint. One of yours?"

He nodded in the affirmative, his eyes feigning injury

at her mocking tone. Or perhaps, she thought, she really had wounded him.

"Tradition," Steed pronounced seriously, "is all we have, Mrs. Peel."

Was he serious?

"There!" Trubshaw said triumphantly, gazing at the impeccable gentleman Steed represented. A man, he might have said, of his own making. "I hope your shoes and waistcoat please, sir."

"Impeccable, Mr. Trubshaw."

"Quite." Emma saw that the old man couldn't prevent a smile from playing at his lips. "Your items will be delivered to the usual address." He cast a glance at Mrs. Peel, then back at Steed. "And Mrs. Peel's boots, sir?"

"Send them on, Mr. Trubshaw."

The old man nodded and left without comment, the soul of discretion, as Steed adjusted his new waistcoat. "Perfect fit. The man's amazing. You'll appreciate Trubshaw's boots."

"I do hope so. I'm quite particular, you know."

"So I'd gathered," Steed said, with heavy irony.

She knew he had taken her meaning. They held each other's eyes for a moment, then she walked briskly past him, out of the shop and into the weak sun shining on Jermyn Street.

Immediately she'd set foot on the pavement, Emma had the feeling she was being watched. Steed had probably been informed that they would be followed; he certainly seemed unconcerned. There *was* the man in the black trench coat gazing into the shop window opposite. . . .

Steed, following her out the door with a swing of his umbrella, looked at the man dressed for weather and nodded at Emma. "Mother," he said, "suggested we go for a spin."

"Do you always listen to Mother?" Emma asked, teasing.

"That depends. Marvelous weather, though, isn't it? Not the sort of day to be stuck in town. We ought to get away."

" 'We?' " Emma said ironically.

"Yes. Just the two of us. A weekend in the country. Long walks, wind in your hair . . . How about it, Mrs. Peel?" He looked as if he quite liked the idea.

"Depends on what you have in mind." She carefully kept warmth out of her tone.

"I'm a nature lover," he said. "So whatever comes naturally."

Her head whipped round, and he raised his eyebrows at her, once. Forward little beast, wasn't he? But then, she liked a man who didn't dither. She did her best to remain inscrutable as they approached his old green behemoth of a Bentley.

"Shall we take my car?" Steed asked, gesturing toward the antique motor. Emma sighed. The poor man really was desperate for tradition. She wasn't sure the old crate would make it to the countryside.

They hopped into the Bentley. Emma struck a blasé pose with her elbow on the door and looked outward. She still hadn't said anything about the Bentley, not even after their first trip to the Ministry. No doubt he wanted her to be impressed with his silly old car, the way men always did. Boys with toys.

Steed turned the ignition, but the car wouldn't start. "Most odd," he said.

"Rusty, perhaps."

Emma said it with an emphasis on the first word that she hoped would leave him in no doubt of her meaning. She was referring to him and certain aspects of his male prowess.

"Yes. Well. Hope I haven't lost the knack." Steed coaxed the throttle, and the motor revved in response. Rrrrrmmmmmm! He had ignition, and what a powerful ignition it was, he was saying. He looked at her significantly, his eyes hooded.

All right, she thought. Point made.

Off they zoomed at high speed, the car taking off as if it were propelled by rocket fuel. Very much like her own specially modified vehicle. Emma realized there was more to this understated man than met the eye.

Perhaps . . .

CHAPTER SEVEN

If thou more murmur'st, I will rend an oak and peg thee in his knotty entrails till thou hast howl'd away twelve winters.

The Tempest, *William Shakespeare*

The man in the trench coat turned from the shop window opposite Trubshaw's and glared at the speeding car. As they left, his bully boys joined him and watched the elegant boot of the departing vehicle.

"Some car, eh, Bailey?" one of them said in a caustic voice. Bailey, his hair a conscientious imitation of a Beatle mop, his lips pouty, didn't acknowledge the question. His open coat revealed a black polo neck, which matched his soul precisely. Sneering, he plucked a cell phone out of his coat pocket to ring Father. That Peel bird wasn't going to live long enough to squawk.

Back at Hallucinogen Hall, the Prospero Program's top antimatter research scientist, Rupert Fellowes, squirmed in agony. The drugs coursing through his bloodstream tortured him mercilessly. The pain, the deafening music, the horrible visions . . .

They'd come for him as he was enjoying a bacon butty in the comfort of his own flat. He'd never considered himself important enough to be in any danger. Who would be interested in a forty-eight-year-old myopic meteorologist with crooked teeth and halitosis? But from the moment he'd opened the door and the man in the black trench coat had pulled the gun from under his coat, Fellowes knew he was in trouble. Heavy weather indeed.

He'd gone with them, of course—not much else he could do with the barrel of that gun staring him in the face. Everything had gone to pieces all of a sudden, he'd thought in the few frenzied moments it had taken them to bundle him into their car. The Prospero research facility had been blown up—secretly, he'd been glad that he hadn't been on duty at the time of the explosion. And they'd only just worked it all out—he had worked it out, in fact. They knew just how much antimatter to inject and what the results would be. They had produced a safe weapon at last. A perfectly natural weapon, nonviolent in its way, that could prevent war.

Yes, he could be proud of the work to which he'd dedicated his life. But what a horrid way to end it. He had an ominous feeling that he would not leave this bizarre place alive, especially if he continued to refuse to answer the questions the monster posed him about Prospero. But it was unthinkable that he would give away Her Majesty's government secrets. Not at all cricket.

Fellowes tried to focus on the monster dancing in a strange, furry costume near him, but the drugs had affected him. He couldn't seem to see clearly. Nor could he turn his head; it seemed to be in a vise of some sort. He felt the monster come near, humming something. Then it turned a dial on the intravenous mechanism that had been inserted into his arm. They'd put it in before he'd awakened on the couch with that horrid hypnodisc whirling in psychedelic patterns above him.

Somehow the beast had given him drugs that left his mind clear while making his body useless. He could feel his heart racing horribly, as if it might pound out of his chest, and he was panting as if he'd run a mile. Heaven knew that would never happen in real life.

Then he realized that the furry thing had either injected a new drug into the mix or increased the dosage of what he was already getting. He felt his body go wild, his heart palpitating. He wanted to jump out of his skin, and quite believed that he might.

Then came the pain. At first he felt a sort of tingling everywhere, then mild prickling as if he were being stuck by a million pins. Then the pinpoints became knives, and it was all he could do to keep from crying out. He could hear himself moaning, but couldn't control himself any longer . . . perhaps a deinhibitor had been introduced. . . .

Worse . . . that furry monster . . . dancing, dancing, horrible. Cruel. Must . . . resist . . .

"Urrrr! Nnnnnnoooooooooo . . ." he screamed, fearing that he would reveal the Prospero secrets as much as he feared the pain. He gritted his teeth and heard his own scream echo in psychedelic patterns, on and on. . . .

What Fellowes couldn't have known was that his torturer, Sir August de Wynter, knew as much about weather as he did. After all, he'd headed the Prospero Project for years—had been the original project director from its inception. He merely had to make sure that Dr. Peel and the collection of scientists at the Prospero Program hadn't learned anything he hadn't. But he was quite confident. . . .

Dressed in his disguise as the tartan-clad giant teddy

bear, Sir August felt utterly free to be himself. And he was a cruel bastard, but he did love sacred music so. He danced with his special ruby-handled, razor-tipped baton, swaying rhythmically, twirling to massed choirs of recorded angelic music as they blended in exquisite harmony.

As the music swelled, Sir August looked over at the mirrored chamber he'd created for his victims' interrogations. The music was even louder on the special couch where the scientist lay, surrounded by mirrors and spinning, spiral hypnodiscs. Enough to drive anyone round the bend!

Sir August smiled inside his giant teddy bear head; then his smile abruptly faded. Couldn't the bloody idiot stop that *moaning*?! Spineless little twit. Bad breath, too.

Suppressing his irritation, Sir August twirled and conducted the heavenly voices in the crowning, frenzied final chorus of *Alleluia!* that echoed endlessly in Bach-like complexity and splendor. No sense in letting this fool ruin his music. Sir August glanced down at the pale, skinny scientist on the special couch, the straps and head clamp keeping him where the drugs could affect him best.

Who could withstand those infinite, pulsating psychedelic patterns, with their ability to confuse and coerce? And with the hallucinogenic cocktail he'd administered this poor berk, the man would soon be begging to tell everything he knew. Yes, his intimate knowledge of hallucinogens had been very useful indeed. He'd been utterly brilliant, too, in designing the special chamber—as brilliant as he was at playing Prospero in his own production of Shakespeare's *Tempest*. He grinned. All the world was *his* stage.

Sir August continued to twirl, losing himself in the music, conducting the masterpiece blasting from his massive floor-to-ceiling speakers with manic ferocity, as if his life depended upon it. Sweat trickled down his back inside the suit. The scientist let out a particularly prolonged scream of agony, and it finally ruined Sir August's fun.

"So bloody tiresome!" Having lost his patience for good, he pointed his baton at the scientist. He stretched out one massive baton-wielding paw, and in perfect time with the music, rhythmically cut and slashed his victim's cheeks with the jeweled baton, drawing beads of blood. The man, who was shaking like a leaf, whimpered and moaned. Such an inferior creature. As the music built to a climax, Sir August whacked the scientist on the nose.

"You *know* what I want to know," he said, as if reprimanding a recalcitrant child.

The scientist only moaned more loudly, which didn't improve Sir August's mood. Furious, Sir August kicked the hypnodisc rotator, which only spun the spiral nightmare-inducer faster. The scientist began to whimper, his body shaking with the effort of holding out. At last, Sir August noted with glee, he could bear it no more. Trembling violently, helplessly, he began to mumble secrets, barely able to pour the words out fast enough to appease the amphetamines that mingled with the other drugs in his bloodstream. . . .

"Ahhh! I . . . we . . . oh . . . in the production of . . . of . . . antimatter, the . . . the ratio of pro . . . protons to ions . . ."

Sir August, singing and dancing, rolled his r's as he sang triumphantly, "Protons to ions . . ."

The scientist continued, desperate. He was blowing like a racehorse. ". . . is . . . is equal to the mass of cloud pre . . . pressure calculated by the Fermetti principle. Using . . . using 'e' as the b-b-base . . ."

" 'E' as the base," Sir August echoed, relishing the intense choral music that soared majestically, utterly overwhelming the scientist. Having got what he wanted— the knowledge that Prospero had gone no further than

he himself had—he listened contentedly for a moment.
On an elegiac climax, complete with soaring violins, he
raised his razor-point baton in ecstasy. It glinted dangerously in the strobe light for a moment; then he plunged
it down, deep into Fellowes' tortured breast.

Steed pulled off the road into a field without explanation. He felt Mrs. Peel's eyes on him, questioning, as he
brought the car to a stop. He saw with satisfaction that
according to plan, when they sat down in the tall grass it
would provide quite an effective privacy screen.

With interest he watched Mrs. Peel survey the waving
heads of the grass around them, hanging heavy with
seed. "Lovely field," she commented. "Do you fancy a
roll in the hay?"

Steed smiled at her. Little did she know how close
she'd come to the truth. But he had rather hoped to
cloak his amorous intentions behind the excuse of stopping for a picnic lunch.

"Mrs. Peel, you never cease to amaze. Surely you
didn't think I would expect you to embark on an adven-
ture of this sort without sufficient sustenance?" He
opened his door, stepped out into the tall grass, and
lifted two wicker picnic hampers out of the backseat.
Steed felt Mrs. Peel's eyes on him as he set off through
the grass, looking for the ideal spot. He heard her car
door close; she was coming after him.

"Ah, here we are," he said, plopping the hampers
down on the ground. He saw Mrs. Peel approach with a
look that said she was both amused and skeptical. As he
lifted out a huge white linen tablecloth and spread it
with a flourish, matting down a rectangle of grass, Steed
hoped that Brenda had lived up to her usual standard.
For years, now, she had never failed him on these occa-
sions. She visited Fortnum and Mason to provision him

for these on-the-job outdoor expeditions, returning
with hampers bulging with all the best England had to
offer (well, admittedly, the best of Europe as well).

Steed enjoyed the way Mrs. Peel watched his every
move, sitting cross-legged on the blanket as he un-
packed the hampers.

"Foie gras," he said, placing the small pot on the
cloth. "Water biscuits. Brie. French loaf. Salmon terrine.
Quiche Lorraine. Potted prawns. Salad with blue cheese,
vinaigrette, and avocado pears. Strawberries . . . black-
berries . . . cream. Ripe peaches. And rum truffles, of
course."

"Well," she said with a smirk. "I suppose we'll muddle through somehow." She watched as he laid out two
Wedgewood china plates and two sets of heavy sterling
cutlery.

He opened the second hamper, which was devoted
exclusively to a large quantity of ice coddling a bottle of
Veuve Cliquot. He grimaced inwardly at the thought of
the French word for "widow" in the name. It was unlike
Brenda not to have considered that. He hoped Mrs. Peel
wouldn't be put off by it. Brenda had put the usual two
heavy Waterford Powerscourt champagne flutes in atop
the bottle, cradled in several linen serviettes.

"First things first," Steed said, plucking out the glasses,
handing them to Mrs. Peel, and pulling the champagne
bottle out of the hamper. He unscrewed the wire cage
that restrained the cork, placing it carefully in the hamper. If nothing else, he was meticulous. Not for him the
casual slovenliness of some bachelors.

Steed tossed one of the linen serviettes over the top
of the orange-labeled bottle, and worked the cork upward with his thumbs. The gas escaping from the bottle
made a satisfying, muffled *thunk* as the cork blew. Since
it had been properly chilled, there was no unseemly
frothing of bubbles down the side. Steed filled both

glasses, returned the bottle to its ice, and took a glass to Mrs. Peel.

"To Her Majesty, the Queen," he said, holding his glass in front of him.

Mrs. Peel reached her glass out, touched it to his. Her eyes sparkled. "Her Majesty, the Queen," she said, and tipped her glass back. Steed hoped the bubbles tickled her nose as enticingly as they did his. He always felt his senses were heightened by fine champagne. This was a good vintage, he noted, with just the right toasty aroma and miniscule bubbles.

Upon lowering his champagne flute Steed was disconcerted to note that Mrs. Peel was watching him—again with that unreadable smirk. He covered his discomfort, asking, "Something wrong? Is the champagne not to your liking? I realize the selection of food is limited, but . . . ?"

She seemed to be deep in thought as she studied him, and didn't respond immediately. This was yet another quality of hers that he prized. She didn't feel a need to babble continuously, to cover silence. A rare quality in a woman.

Then she spoke—thoughtfully and deliberately. "Everything is . . . quite sufficient, Steed."

Something about the way she was looking at him, and the arched eyebrow over her left eye, suggested that she wasn't referring to the comestibles.

"I am delighted to hear it," he said mildly, hardly knowing how to receive such a compliment. To cover his surprise, he dipped a knife into the pâté and meticulously plastered a torn piece of French bread with it. He was aware that she, too, had busied herself with food, though he didn't look directly at her for several moments. She actually did fancy him, he thought. In a corner of his soul that had never been explored—he had never dared open that last stronghold against vulnerability to anyone—he felt something come to life.

They dined, then, in the most extraordinary silence. It was the most romantic, alluring, titillating meal of his life. He realized he'd never had a silent meal before, other than when he'd been alone. He watched her eat and drink; she watched him. Steed had never felt so attracted to anyone in his life. Emma—what a thrill to call her by her Christian name!—was a mere three feet away across the cloth, her lips moist with champagne, her catsuit accentuating all the right curves and indentations.

Between the perfect balance of the champagne, the yeastiness of the French loaf, the richness of the pâté, not to mention *Emma* . . . Steed found his senses stimulated beyond all reason. When Emma finally bit into a peach after sampling the other delicacies, he actually blinked. But he wouldn't allow himself further breaches of inscrutability. There was too much at stake.

Pouring more champagne in their glasses, he told himself that when the time came to, er, *connect* with Mrs. Emma Peel, the experience would be extraordinary. He would most definitely have to wait until the right time; it wouldn't do to rush things. That might ruin everything. So until they both deemed it to be the appropriate moment, the suspense was almost more than he could bear. It was delicious, rapturous . . . cruel.

They stared at each other and drank the last of their champagne. Neither of them spoke another word.

CHAPTER EIGHT

How now? moody? What is't thou canst demand?
The Tempest, *William Shakespeare*

The Bentley purred down a single track lane in Cambridgeshire. Steed said to Emma, "Press that button, would you? Tea?"

Emma obeyed without comment. A dashboard compartment opened in front of her, revealing a silver tea service. A samovar of tea fed into the Wedgewood teapot, which then poured accurately into china cups.

"Is the pot warm?"

He seemed to catch her meaning and glanced at her. "Always."

"Milk?" Emma inquired, looking sideways at him.

He shook his head once, quickly. "Lemon. Just a twist." His words hit her hard, actually disconcerting her for a moment. It was just how her husband had taken his tea, before that fateful trip to the Amazon.

Was it breaking her lifelong pledge to be interested in

this John Steed? After what had happened at the picnic,
that most extraordinary of all meals, she wasn't alto-
gether certain she had a choice. She had always believed
in putting the past behind her, and in taking risks. She
was certainly doing that.

But really, she told herself, she was in no position to
be interested in anyone. She could be a dangerous mental case. The best thing she could do for Steed might be
to escape from his classic dinosaur of a car and never see
him again.

Nevertheless, Emma plucked a lemon wedge from a
bowl that brimmed over with them and briefly squeezed
it over Steed's tea before passing him the cup and saucer.

"No cakes, I'm afraid," Steed said apologetically.
"You don't mind roughing it, do you?"

"On the contrary." There was a smile behind her
words. "But shouldn't we be making plans for tonight?"

"Oh we are, Mrs. Peel. We are. Thought we'd have
time to pay a social visit. Since we happened to be
passing."

"Mmm. I thought as much. Anyone in particular?"

"Sir August de Wynter. Former Ministry man. Head
of Special Projects, ran our Strategic Deception Initia-
tive. He's retired now. Very rich, very odd."

"Intriguing. A wealthy recluse?"

Emma saw Steed concentrate on something in the
rearview mirror. She looked in the side mirror. A car.
Was it trailing them? He put his foot down, and with his
finger engaged the superthrottle. The Bentley took off
like the TGV.

When Emma had managed to lift her head away from
the back of the seat, where it had been pressed during
Steed's acceleration, she turned to look at him again.

He carried on the conversation as if he hadn't just
propelled them through the English countryside at
nearly one hundred miles per hour with a blast of rocket
fuel. "More interesting than that. Sir August's a fanatical

meteorologist. Runs in the family. Mother called April. Sisters: May, June . . ."

"July, August?" Emma finished. "The family does seem to have weather on the brain. Any other vices?"

"All of a piece, really. Sir August's chairman of BROLLY. . . ."

Emma looked at him askance. He *couldn't* be serious.

"Yes, the British Royal Organization for Lasting Liquid Years. A private group recruiting top scientists." He did seem to be serious, Emma thought. "Thinks British weather has been tampered with by . . . aliens. All very hush-hush. Not too keen on him at the Ministry. Mother tells me he left under—"

"A cloud?" she supplied blandly.

"Naturally." He turned and smiled at her. "If it wouldn't be too much bother, do you suppose you might charm him a little?"

"I'll see what I can do." She crossed her arms in front of her.

"More tea?"

"No, thanks."

"I meant for me," he said, sounding forlorn. "But never mind. Here we are."

Ahead of them, gates swung open to reveal a vast, strange house studded with towers and turrets, like the fantasy of a madman. *King Ludwig's castle in Neuschwanstein couldn't hold a candle to this,* Emma thought. It was immense, evil, and symptomatic of a brilliant mind gone wrong. Steed stopped the Bentley at the gate, but kept the motor running.

"I'll snoop around," he said. "You distract him."

Right, Emma thought. "And how do you propose that I do that?"

"Try small talk."

"Ah, yes. The weather."

"Or . . . perhaps something more feminine. A woman's

touch . . ." He turned, receiving the full effect of the look Emma trained on him. "That should do the trick."

"Think so? Your confidence is overwhelming."

"Such modesty," he said.

"A minor talent. Or hadn't you noticed?"

Steed didn't comment, but she couldn't blame him. Perhaps the fencing episode had been more of an embarrassment to the man than she'd realized. He dropped her in the drive, near Hallucinogen Hall, as an engraved stone at the gate had proclaimed. She set off into the courtyard, treading on white pea gravel past potted topiaries, and he drove off in the car to explore.

Emma walked past a mechanical peacock, which fanned its tail as she passed. She had no way of knowing that its silent camera was whirring to life.

Steed left the car on the drive and hiked off into the grounds of the Hall, casting a glance toward the house to see if he could spot Emma. She had accepted her assignment quite cooperatively, he thought. She was reputed to have excellent skills at this sort of interpersonal espionage. It was one of the things about her he found so intriguing.

If she *were* in bed with Sir August de Wynter— metaphorically speaking, of course—this visit to his home would be nothing more than a chance for her to confer with her cohorts. But he'd watched her carefully as they'd approached the house. He was quite certain this was as new to her as it was to him. But she was so cool, so unflappable . . . it was hard to tell.

If she were on the other side, he'd have to watch his back. This little outing would be a fine opportunity for them to dispose of him.

As he walked off toward the outbuildings of the Hall, swinging his umbrella, he chuckled to himself at the way she'd been caught off guard by the Bentley. He loved to

surprise people with that booster engine. Never failed to
entertain.

But in the next moment he frowned, recognizing a
complication. Swatting his umbrella against the tall, un-
mown grass, he had to admit he'd never felt this way
about anyone who might potentially be a psychopath—
or, perhaps worse yet, an enemy agent. The way her hair
blew in the wind, the sadness in her eyes, the sparks of
intelligence that flew from them—she, Mrs. Emma Peel,
was the woman he'd always dreamed of. She could even
beat him at fencing.

He'd have to watch his back, all right. Not to mention his heart.

Unbeknownst to Emma, the eyes she'd felt outside Trubshaw's were on her again. As she climbed the front steps
to the Hall's massive door, Bailey watched her with narrowed eyes.

He saw her ring the bell, saw the butler greet her. She
was in. He took a handheld radio out of his pocket and
switched it on. Everything was going according to plan.

Emma followed the elderly butler down a central corridor. Without explanation, he turned and handed her an
umbrella.

"Thank you," she said politely, and kept moving after
him down the hallway. Hallucinogen Hall was one of
the great stately homes of England, and though the exterior was wildly out of whack with anyone's idea of attractive design, the interior was pleasant enough. It was
an eclectic mix of Georgian, Gothic, and Jacobean styles,
but, oddly, it worked. The rooms she and the butler
passed were duly littered with antiques, fine artwork,
and paneled walls.

Intrigued, Emma noticed the corridor was garlanded

with strange plants and flowers. In particular, she was captivated by a pair of sensuous, oversized orchids.

"Curious," she commented.

The butler looked over his shoulder and shot a distracted "Yes, miss," in her direction before continuing.

"Missus."

He failed to acknowledge her correction, but she was used to that. At the end of the corridor, Emma saw a set of double doors. From them, the voice of Pavarotti singing Puccini echoed loudly, bouncing down the corridor. Curious, Emma followed the elderly man closer and closer, until finally he opened the doors to reveal nothing less than an interior rain forest.

The butler left her, in rather an unseemly hurry, she thought, after he'd taken one long, last look at her face. She wondered what that was all about. Shrugging, she moved into the room, gazing in wonder at tangled trees and creepers. She understood the issuance of the umbrella, now; the rain misted in a tropical monsoon. As if in a tympanic background to the Puccini, thunder rolled.

"Hello?" she ventured, putting her umbrella up.

There was no reply. As she stalked further into the room, looking for de Wynter, she saw ahead, through the jungle mist, a large shadow cast on the wall. The shadow spun wildly, dervishlike, singing along to Pavarotti's perfect rendition of an intensely seductive Puccini aria.

"Talor dal mio forziere Ruban tutti I gioielli Due ladri: gli occhi belli . . ."

With irritation Emma noted the voice was slightly off-key. To someone with her perfect pitch, that was a sacrilege. Sighing, she decided that this clinched it. She would have no difficulty killing him, should it prove necessary. Desecrating Puccini, after all . . . not to mention her good friend Luciano . . .

She pushed past dripping branches, through the rain

forest, into the heart of darkness. On and on, through the damp tangle of vines and creepers until . . . suddenly, behind her, branches rustled unnaturally. She wheeled, knocking into something hard as a hand reached up and clasped her around the neck like a serpent.

Startled, Emma looked up to see a handsome, charismatic man in the rain and the mist. *Sir August,* she thought. Well, at least he'd given up singing for the moment.

"Peel," he said, drawing the name out as he looked into her eyes. "Emma Peel."

Thunder rolled as if on cue; lightning flashed, illuminating his glinting eyes and wicked smile. He was a mature man, perhaps fifty-five, but in his case age had contributed to his good looks and appeal. He was at least six feet tall, and powerfully built. The bulges of firm muscles showed beneath his clothing, and the muscles of his face were taut. He radiated sexuality. She had the impression he would have all the attributes of a younger man, and a few more as well—the kind that could only be obtained through vast experience.

But for all that, he was still a maniac, she thought. No question.

"You're all wet," she said.

His smile faded dangerously.

"Have we met?" she asked, feigning confusion. "Or is it just the rain that's familiar?"

He moved under her umbrella with intimacy. Their eyes locked together. There was a sudden blinding flash of light, and Emma jumped as a bolt of lightning struck them. She was looking at him when the bolt traveled through her umbrella shaft, and was appalled to see that he seemed gleeful as the current flowed through him, his mouth open in a wide grin. Momentarily stunned, feeling disoriented, she dropped the handle in the aftermath of the jolt. He caught the crook before it could fall, and held it above her head as he watched her with interest, solicitously putting an arm around her.

The hazards of playing with the weather, she thought. *And lunatics.*

It took her a moment to recover. She was not quite herself, and still a bit stunned as he said, his mouth close to her ear, "We share a passion, I believe." He kissed her hand. Oh no, she thought. Not this. "I always admire a woman who's meteorologically inclined."

"Mutual, I'm sure," she played along. "The thrill of the monsoon."

"Mmm. Even as a boy, when Nana taught me the naming of clouds."

"Cumulus," Emma said softly.

"Yes . . ." he breathed.

"Stratocumulus," she moaned.

"Oh, yes . . ." His chest rose and fell with each rasping breath.

'Nimbus . . ." she whispered, letting the *s* hiss out seductively.

Without warning, he threw Emma's umbrella into the jungle behind them. Raising his bushy eyebrows at her, he said with meaning, "I've discovered nothing beats a good lashing."

Kinky, she thought, raising one eyebrow in return. *This could get interesting.*

"Take India," he continued. "Or Singapore. You can have a good ten inches overnight."

"Ah," she said. "Yes. Well. Too true. Nothing like a good lashing."

He led her out of the rain. "This way," Sir August said. He turned and looked at her as he went on. "One should never fear being wet, Emma."

Such familiarity, she thought. And did he mean that the way she thought he did? Good Lord. Perhaps he was obsessed with sex as well as the weather.

Still in the rain forest, but in a microclimate where it

had stopped raining for the moment, Sir August snatched
up a thick white towel from a wicker table. It was em-
broidered beautifully in forest-green floss with "de W",
and a family crest consisting of a cloud pierced by a
golden lightning bolt. *Not unlike the Prospero logo,*
Emma thought.

He moved closer. "Let me give you a hand."

Standing behind her, Sir August eagerly rubbed
Emma's hair dry. She felt his strength, knew that with
his manic intensity he could be a formidable opponent.
She also felt his sexuality, his twistedness, as his strong
arms embraced her from behind. He took the towel
from her hair and started down her backside with delicacy, patting her leather suit dry.

*Nothing like a bit of cold water on an overheated
furnace,* Emma thought. She burst out, deliberately sudden, "These rapid climate changes. The Ministry needs
some answers."

Disgusted, Sir August stopped patting her dry and
hissed, "The *Ministry* . . ."

"Do you mind?" Emma asked sweetly, smiling as she
turned to face him.

Almost to himself, he mumbled, "I wouldn't mind
anything with you." But to Emma, he said meekly, "Very
well."

Emma watched as Sir August inspected her wistfully,
smelling, caressing, becoming intoxicated by her. He
continued to dry her off, but they both knew the exer-
cise was no more than an excuse to massage every inch
of her body with the towel. Emma wondered if Steed
would consider this charming enough.

"I need a specialist opinion," Emma began. "Theo-
retically speaking, if I wanted to alter cloud patterns,
how would I power it? By microtransmission?"

Sir August moved down to her knees, an admittedly
tender zone, even through leather—especially on the
back of her legs. She frowned in concentration as he

knelt behind her, kissing her on the crease behind her knees, then gently patting off the moisture in a way that titillated. How on earth did he know? she wondered.

"I've been thinking," she began again, closing her eyes briefly. "The military applications were never looked into. After the cold war—"

He was panting. "The hot and cold war."

"An outdated theory. Intriguing but possible."

He looked up briefly, hesitating. "Nothing's impossible. Only mathematically improbable, my dear Dr. Peel."

Emma broke off curtly, twisting out of his caress. "Dry enough now, don't you think?"

Sir August, only momentarily deterred, agreeably changed course. He led her to his prize orchids, which sat under huge magnifying glasses.

"Look here," he said pointing. "The twisted labellum. Note the upturned apiculus on the dorsal sepal. A genetic impossibility. This flower should not exist. Yet here it is. I did it. Beautiful, no?" He stroked it with affection.

Definitely twisted, Emma thought. *A real bent twig.*

"Touch it, Dr. Peel," he urged, looking into her eyes.

She crossed her arms firmly beneath her breasts. "I'm wasting my time."

"Please," Sir August implored, almost tenderly. "Touch it."

"No. I'm sorry to have troubled you," she said, making as if to walk away. "It's obvious you know nothing."

The remark stung him. Old resentments and scorn flooded back until his rage boiled over. He stepped close and leaned over Emma, arms rigid at his sides.

"I—I know nothing?!" He snorted, furious. "I have forgotten more than those fools at the Ministry ever knew. The ratio of protons to ions? *Me.* The entire microtransmission theory? *Me.* I did it all. *My* way. They said I was mad. . . ."

A sudden noise from the double doors startled them both. They turned to look, and saw the butler pushing a tea trolley toward them.

"Ah, Farthing. Tea?" Sir August seemed to recover his equilibrium at the thought of the familiar ritual. He went to meet the white-haired retainer, who was placing the tea trolley near the picture window at the side of the room.

The butler whispered something to Sir August as Emma walked over to join him by the window. When the old man had delivered his message, he retreated in haste.

Sir August poured the tea, staring out at the rain.

"Perhaps your friend would like to join us?" Sir August turned on her suddenly, giving her a feral look that caught her off guard.

"My friend?"

"Hmm. Some very nasty weather about." He looked rabid, Emma thought, though his words were civil enough.

"Ah . . . Perhaps he's lost."

"I don't think so. We don't get many trespassers up here." His face was tight.

"Oh? Why?"

"We shoot them." He held up a teaspoonful of white granules. "Sugar?"

Sir August gazed out the window, and Emma followed his stare. She felt the first faint stirrings of concern for Steed's welfare.

CHAPTER NINE

For still 'tis beating in my mind ... your reason for raising this ... storm?

The Tempest, *William Shakespeare*

Beneath the NO TRESPASSERS sign outside, Steed looked up as it began to hail. He put up his Trubshaw's umbrella and headed for a red phone box not far away. The hail threatened to rip the oiled canvas cloth on his umbrella to shreds. He couldn't think when he'd been out in such foul weather.

"I say, this is a bit much," he muttered.

As he reached the relative safety of the phone box, the storm whipped up, hammering against the glass. The telephone began to ring. Steed looked at it curiously, picked it up and heard someone squawking down the line at him.

"Hello? Hello?" The male voice on the other end was incredulous. "Who the hell . . . ? Who is this? You must get out of the test area. I repeat, *leave the area*!"

The line went dead. Steed retreated further into the

corner of the phone box, covering his head with his arms. The wind speed increased until it swirled with almost tornadic force, picking up rocks like bits of straw and tossing them against the phone box. The glass panels shattered, raining shards on him. Rocks, branches, and a hail of other debris flew into the box. Finally the box itself was lifted right off the ground, spinning like a farmhouse in a tornado.

"How extraordinary!" he exclaimed as he hung on to the telephone, doing his best to stay in the minimal shelter. But as the box landed on the ground again, his head bashed hard against the metal structure. He saw stars, then sank, inert, to the floor of the box.

Steed groaned. What a shocking headache . . . Had it been champers at Boodle's again with the lads? The Boat Race Ball? Ah. No. It came back now with brutal clarity—stormy weather. He opened his eyes and put a hand to his head, which was disturbingly bowlerless. Something sticky in his hair. But then . . . coming to complete awareness, he realized he was sitting in the middle of a giant snowdrift. Only the scant protection of what was left of the phone box had saved him from complete burial in the snow.

Not believing his eyes, he got to his feet, dusted off the bowler on the floor next to him and set it firmly where it belonged. He opened the door and stepped out into three and a half feet of snow. Its cold penetrated his shoes and trousers immediately, began to freeze his feet. He squinted; the sun was blinding, reflecting off a myriad of crystals. Steed thought he might be dreaming, something to do with the whack on the head.

But as he stood pondering the wonder of it all, shielding his eyes with a hand, he saw a lone figure on the horizon. *It's Emma, coming to rescue me,* he thought.

But it was all so white-on-white, he couldn't be sure. Shaking his head gently, he looked at the snow in front of him, picked up a handful of the stuff and let it sift through his fingers.

The figure seemed to move toward him as he watched; a puff of snow erupted on the horizon. "A mirage, perhaps," Steed murmured, as he made out a sled of huskies and a white-fur-clad Eskimo mushing toward him. He tried to make out who was on the sled, but couldn't see more than the full-body white fur and goggles.

The sled stopped in front of him and its rider dismounted, completely swathed in white fur. Looking down, he saw a kinky boot of white fur, crisscrossed with buckled straps. As his gaze climbed upward, he saw a tall woman clad in a mixture of Inuit and Parisian couture. Zipped into that figure-hugging cocoon, she may well have been Emma, but he couldn't tell because of the goggles masking her face. Her hair was hidden beneath a white fur hood attached to the cocoon.

"Mrs. Peel?" he tried.

The slinky Eskimo vixen drew nearer, her identity a mystery. From the sled, she quickly took up a crossbow, aimed, and fired before Steed fully realized what was happening. "That'd be a five in the lab," he murmured, and dodged as he heard a harpoon whining, then thudding into the phone box. He saw its jagged teeth rip into the red metal, just inches away. He thought for a nanosecond, then ran.

It was difficult, wading through four feet of snow. The woman gained on him, and in no time at all, he found himself hopelessly trapped between a brick wall and a barn. A brick wall and a barn? They hadn't *been* there earlier, he was sure. . . .

However they'd done it, he was well and truly cornered. Most unlikely, he thought. But the game was up.

He turned to face the woman, shivering in the snow. She whipped off her goggles, revealing herself to be none other than Emma Peel.

Confused, Steed focused on her. "Is that you, Mrs. Peel?"

The woman moved closer, an eerie glint in her eye. She unzipped the top third of the long zipper down her front, and produced a thirty-eight-caliber gun. She pointed it directly at Steed, aiming quickly and competently, he noted, not even squinting down the barrel. She appeared to be training it on his heart. Well, that was appropriate enough. All right, he could add shooting to her evidently endless repertoire of skills. She didn't have to prove it.

In disbelief, he watched as she poised her forefinger on the trigger. He said, "Manners, Mrs. Peel. Manners."

She fired. The sound of the single shot was muffled by the snow.

The impact threw Steed backward. Stunned, he lay staring at the now-clear sky. He'd so been looking forward to getting to know Emma Peel better. . . . If she didn't like him, she hadn't had to *shoot* him. . . .

Steed's eyes closed.

"Steed . . . Steed?" It was her voice . . . Emma's.

He flinched, expecting another shot. When it didn't come, his eyes blinked open. She was leaning over him, looking frightfully concerned. That was odd, he thought. The last time he'd seen her she'd plugged him full of lead.

Turning his head to the side, away from her, he saw the same landscape by the phone box, but without snow. He looked at her again, suspiciously—only she seemed different now, back to the Emma Peel he knew. Something about her eyes; not at all like before. She'd got out of the white fur, and was back in that stunning second skin of white leather. And leaning over him as she was . . . well, it was quite a sight.

With an effort, he brought his eyes back up to her face, blinking as he tried to focus. She looked so concerned . . . hard to believe she had shot him. But she was certain to finish him off now, and he . . . felt . . . so strange . . .

"What happened?" she asked, leaning over him, looking almost . . . tender. He tried to speak, but nothing happened. He wanted to believe that she cared about him. . . . would come to his rescue. Such a nice dream.

A shame she was so desperately, pathologically psychotic. Father had obviously been right.

Then it all faded away again.

All in the line of duty, Emma told herself as she got her arms around her injured colleague, draped him over her shoulder, and trudged back to the Bentley. She had put the ridiculous bowler on her own head to get it back to the car. Steed's head lolled and bounced as she carried him like a sack of flour. He was a bit unwieldy because of his height, but it was doable. A jolly good thing she'd kept up with her weight-lifting regimen.

If the fencing had embarrassed him, Emma thought, this would really put his tail between his legs. While he was still flat on his back she'd checked his pulse, which seemed to be all right. When she'd looked him over for injuries, she'd found a nasty gash on his head and a lump the size of an English rose. After she'd touched his hair, he'd actually seemed to come around for a moment. A bit sad, really—he'd looked frightened of her. Evidently he believed that she had destroyed Prospero headquarters . . . as perhaps she had.

She shifted his weight, making for the car with all due speed, feeling that it somewhat overstepped the bounds of their working relationship to have him riding on her shoulder as he was. He'd actually looked rather sweet, as if he were sleeping there on the grass. She'd found it disturbing that his extremities were so cold when she'd taken his hand; she'd massaged his hands and feet, hoping to stimulate the circulation. When she did, she'd found his hands appealing, the fingers long and slender, as if perhaps he played the piano. Hands were everything in a man, she believed. A sign of what he was really made of.

So what on earth was wrong with the man? She'd dress the head wound back at her house and ice the swelling. Perhaps it was just the bump on the head. As she approached the Bentley, she glanced back at the Hall. No trouble from that quarter—not now, at any rate. Sir August de Ranged's ardor had rather cooled after he'd spotted Steed outside, and he had waved her away with a dismissive twist of his powerful hand. She'd taken the opportunity to scarper and had found Steed off in the east forty near a barn, of all things. Odd, she hadn't seen the barn when they'd approached earlier. . . .

"Oof!" She flipped Steed into the backseat, taking care that she didn't damage him further. She arranged his body so that it looked reasonably comfortable, grappled for the keys in the pockets of his trousers—*much* too intimate, that—then hopped in the driver's seat. She was going to enjoy a spin in his souped-up bag of bolts, though she'd never let him know it. She knew a thing or two about cars. . . .

She had no sooner put the keys into the ignition when Steed groaned from the backseat. Quickly, she turned to look at him. His eyes were closed, his expression pained, and he rolled his head back and forth as if trou-

bled. She felt such a sudden upwelling of empathy—
or *tenderness*, perhaps—that she abruptly turned away
from him. It was no time to go soft.

"Start the car, Mrs. Peel," she ordered herself. She
turned his key in the ignition with determination. The
car fired up, and she floored the accelerator. They were
off to London.

It was the sound of clacking heels on metal that eventually woke him. He heard their incessant *click-clack*ing
and thought, *for goodness sake, why doesn't she take off
those shoes?* On the other hand, he thought, Emma—
when she wasn't gunning him down in full Eskimo
regalia—did look rather fetching in those heels.

He opened his eyes slowly, blinking. Bright. White.
Like the snow. He squinted, then closed them again.
Moments later, his mind seemed to clear and he opened
them again. Not snow; white paint. He was in a strange,
very white bed, in a strange bedroom. It was the ultra-
modern style of the room that made him feel he was still
in some bizarre dreamland. The ceiling was thirty feet
high—odd, for a bedroom, and *everything* was white.
Everything, that is, except for his umbrella, leaning
against the bedside table, and his bowler, which rested
atop the table. The walls, the bed, the duvet, the roses
cascading in an arch over the doorway, the chair, and
the round, white-damask-covered table—all white. Where
was he . . . ?

Steed hoisted himself up into a sitting position as he
heard the heels come *click-clack*ing in his direction. He
did a double-take as Emma, his would-be assassin—and
from all appearances, rescuer as well—appeared in the
doorway. This time she stood out starkly against the
white room in an all-black, one-piece catsuit with an exaggerated zipper right down the front—neck to, well,

the nether reaches. He stared at her dubiously as she clattered over, delivering an all-white tea set to his bedside, next to the white fruit bowl which contained nearly white grapes.

"Tea," she said cheerfully, apparently disregarding the fact that she had tried to kill him. At least she had failed. Aha! He had her there. "With lemon." She picked a grape and held it out to him. "Grape?"

Steed shook his head slowly, his eyes narrowed.

"I bought them specially," she said, trying a smile. "Mind the pips."

Steed gave her no reaction whatsoever, and she shrugged, leaving him to his tea. She *click-clack*ed across the metal walkway leading from the room, wearing high-heeled black boots. Highly unconventional. She then proceeded noisily down the stairs, chattering all the while.

"I hope you don't mind me taking liberties. I had to tuck you up in bed. You didn't seem in very good shape when I found you."

Steed climbed out of bed and took stock of his surroundings, lifting a hand to the bandage on his head as he walked to the metal bridge and peered down at her.

Emma began to play an all-white grand piano. Bach. His favorite. Perfect tempo, perfect execution, he noted. It took a person of precision to do credit to Bach, he thought with approval. And he'd noticed her hands from the start. Hands always indicated the sort of person you were dealing with, he thought. It was as if a person's essence seeped into their fingers. Hers were both strong and slender, with useful fingernails. He'd guessed that she might be a pianist, because her nails weren't horribly long and painted.

"I was frozen stiff," he said, warmed by the music. He watched her hands. "Now I feel much revived."

"Not me you should thank for that."

"Actually, I wasn't about to. I recall a very strange thing." He hesitated; the Bach continued coolly. "You tried to shoot me, didn't you?"

"How absurd," she said, still playing. "I would never shoot you—at least, not without my reasons."

As she pretended to concentrate on the complicated fingering required in the two-part invention, Emma shuddered inwardly. *Had* she shot Steed? Perhaps she'd fallen prey to another psychotic episode sometime after the aborted tea with de Wynter. She felt herself grow cold, felt him staring at her from above. It was all she could do to keep her fingers moving in the complex patterns required by her favorite composer.

"I remember it all too clearly," Steed said, steel in his voice. "One shot to the heart. You were looking right at me. Luckily . . ." She looked up at him as he reached into his waistcoat and pulled the bullet from his clothing, near his heart. "My Trubshaw waistcoat was bulletproof."

Emma sniggered, feigning flippancy as her fingers flew over the keys. "Silly me. And I thought you were just overdressed. 'Be prepared,' is that your motto?"

"I thought it best to take precautions, yes. One never knows." Steed started down the stairs.

"I suppose Mother warned you about women like me." Emma was pleased to note that her voice didn't betray her doubts about herself.

"Until now, I didn't think there *were* women like you."

Emma flinched inwardly at the possible truth of that statement. She thought that there were, in all probability, very few psychotic, sociopathic doctors of meteorology who had once been secret agents and therefore knew how to kill with devastating accuracy. Fortunately, she was good at these slick comebacks. "Obviously. I'm the sort that doesn't take no for an answer."

"Oh, but I should think that would depend on the question, Mrs. Peel." He was silent for a moment. "I say, you *are* definitely Mrs. Peel, aren't you?" She thought she heard something like hope, or perhaps the least bit of desperation, in his voice.

Frostiness was the only way to combat the emotions she felt. She didn't know, after all, that she *was* always Mrs. Peel. Perhaps she turned into Mrs. Hyde every evening when the moon came out.

"You're delirious," she said icily. "I should have abandoned you. Nursing an invalid isn't my idea of fun after all. I could have taken up any amount of offers. . . ."

"And?" He stepped off the stairway onto the ground floor and crossed to the piano, noting the desperate state of his trousers. They needed a press immediately. It struck him then that in order for her to have got him, wrinkled trousers and all, to her flat, she'd had to somehow get him first to the car, then upstairs to the bed. And she'd been staring at him for God knew how long, no doubt while his mouth was open. He felt his eyes widen in mortification. He closed them for a moment.

"I did find a clue at Sir August's," she was saying. "You see, Steed"—Emma paused for a moment, as Steed hung on her every word—"a woman's touch."

Impressed, Steed watched Mrs. Peel's hands glide expertly over the keyboard—until suddenly she sat back on the bench and folded her hands in her lap. The keys continued to move in their computer-programmed rendition of the Bach two-part invention as Steed watched. Emma smiled archly at him.

Damn, Steed thought. Fooled again. This woman was dangerous, indeed. Even her *hands* had fooled him. Strange, that test had never failed before. As Steed watched her with the attitude one would take toward an exotic and dangerous animal, Mrs. Peel walked to a white lacquer table and picked up a toy snow shaker. She turned it over, beckoning him to join her. Warily, he stepped closer and saw a sticker on the underside.

"Wonderland Weather Corporation," he read aloud. Well, hooray. For this child's toy, he'd been utterly humiliated. *It had jolly well better lead somewhere,* he thought.

CHAPTER TEN

What impossible matter will he make easy next?
The Tempest, *William Shakespeare*

Emma pressed the buzzer outside the door, and they heard a click as it was unlocked. Steed pushed it open, and they found themselves inside the reception area of Wonderland Weather. The interior, Emma thought, looked like a bank that catered to the wealthy. The floor was covered with plush blue carpeting, and the walls were covered with huge oil-painted tableaux of clouds, rain, and sun. Emma and Steed looked at each other and approached the receptionist's desk, populated by one very snooty-looking, ski-jump-nosed Sloane Ranger. The sign on her desk proclaimed her to be TAMARA.

"Hello. Wonderland Weather?" Steed was at his most charming, which irritated Emma no end. Why did men always do that with women? Much nicer to women—

and to *strange* women—than they were to men. It always worked, too.

"Yes. May I help you?" Tamara began to warm to him. Emma saw all the signs.

"Do hope so. We've been recommended by a friend who said you'd know all about our problem. We're awfully worried about our roses, you see. . . ."

There it was, Emma thought. She'd known the puppy-dog look would be used eventually, and she hadn't been wrong.

Tamara frowned, eager to help, but confused. She shook her head, and her diamond earrings wobbled. "I don't understand. . . ."

Steed smiled reassuringly and continued. "My colleague and I represent FLORA—Flower Lovers of Ross and Cromarty Association—a very influential group of flower growers working under tremendously adverse conditions. For some years we've been breeding a special rose, the Crimson Monk, until in the past week we've been plagued by ladybirds."

"I thought ladybirds loved roses," Tamara said, smiling tentatively.

"A little *too* much," Steed said. "Now our flower show's coming up, we need a few more warm summer days very quickly—"

"I really don't see how I can help," Tamara said, apologizing.

"You don't?" Steed inquired, wide-eyed. Emma groaned silently. "Haven't you seen a seven-spotted ladybird in the mating season? Speckled grey larvae. A month to pupate, then—no more roses. Voracious . . ."

Steed moved closer. *In for the kill,* thought Emma. She wasn't sure she could bear to watch any more, and snatched up a magazine from a tabletop with a great deal more force than the act required.

"I hope I haven't come to the wrong place." Steed

frowned. Emma knew Tamara would want to relieve his worries, erase that frown. "I was recommended by a member of BROLLY."

Tamara pretended to be utterly confused. *"Brolly?"*

"Don't say you haven't heard of it," Steed said, waving a finger at her in flirtatious reprimand. "I was speaking to my colleague, Sir August—you do know Sir August de Wynter?"

"Of course." Tamara sat up straight and began to look as if she knew where he was leading.

Emma looked up from her yawn-inducing copy of *Cloud Seeding Weekly* as Tamara rose. "This way, please," she said, leading Steed and Emma through a doorway in the wall behind her desk. Emma gave Steed a disgusted look as she passed through the doorway ahead of him. He pretended not to understand. No doubt he was still humiliated over her putting him to bed. In retrospect, if she'd known he was going to be this way about it, she'd have gone a bit further—tucked a teddy in next to him. She smiled at the thought. Oh, well—next time.

Tamara led them into a dimly lit showroom curtained in burgundy velvet. At eye level, glowing glass spheres the size of extra-large fishbowls sat on burgundy velvet-covered pedestals. The walls were decorated with murals of pale blue, cloud-studded English skies.

Tamara beckoned them over to one of the fishbowls as if she were about to share a secret. Each of the glass globes appeared to be a tiny microweather system all its own. The one nearest them was a sunny climate, two more down the line were plagued with snow and rain, respectively.

"Our newest line," Tamara gushed. "Summer or winter, Tuscany or Gstaad. Natural weather delivered down your phone line. All you'll need is a radio transmitter." Tamara looked terrifically pleased with herself and Wonderland Weather.

Steed glowed at her. Emma thought she might be sick. "How real will it feel?" he asked.

"Very," she said, standing closer to him than was strictly necessary. "A whole new line in personalized meteorology. Imagine. An autumn mist, dappled sunshine through an orchard glade, temperature . . ."

"Round sixty-five Fahrenheit?" Steed asked agreeably.

"Whatever you fancy, sir." She meant it most sincerely, Emma thought. Tamara fairly beamed at him.

"Sounds marvelous. A solution to matters meteorological and horticultural. And to my roses." Steed continued to charm Tamara, drawing her near for an intense discussion of his roses while Emma broke away for a bit of snooping.

She looked askance at the trite slogans on placards throughout the showroom: "Be natural. Act natural. Think natural. The natural beauty of Wonderland Weather." Emma stopped and stared at a model in one of the ads that looked exactly like her. Coincidence? She thought not.

The phone rang, interrupting Tamara's burgeoning relationship with Steed.

Disappointed, and flustered, she said, "Oh! One moment. Excuse me." She hurried toward the door to reception.

Steed used his most suggestive tone to murmur, "Hurry back." Emma stared at him, incredulous.

Putty in his hands, Tamara oozed through the doorway, looking back at him with a bedroomy smile. She gave a little wave before disappearing completely.

It took Steed approximately three seconds to grab a doorstop and wedge Tamara's door closed behind her.

"Well," Emma said, watching him, arms akimbo. "I thought I was going to have to duck out the door, leave you two alone together. She was practically salivating."

"All in the line of duty, Mrs. Peel. A bit of masculine

charm, you see . . ." He turned and studied her. "Don't tell me you're jealous?" he said, teasing.

She made a sound of exasperation and headed for a door at the other end of the room labeled "Staff Only." She opened it a crack; peered round. It led to a corridor. She motioned for Steed to follow.

Good, she thought, trying to ignore the ever-so-subtle scent of masculine cologne he wore as he came to stand just behind her. This was what she loved. The thrill of the hunt, the joy of the chase.

On the other side of the wall from Emma and Steed, Sir August the Insane, wearing his tartan teddy disguise, held court in Wonderland Weather's impressive board-room. At a polished cherry table twenty feet long sat eight more teddy bears, each the size of a six-foot-tall man, and each terrifying. It was partly the sinister expressions on the faces of their bear disguises, partly the bizarre pastel colors. Their paws and ears were oversized. Sir August was flanked by the only two nonpastel teddies besides himself: one red bear, one black, clearly his assistants.

The tartan teddy waxed eloquent, clearly enjoying the moment. "Together, we can make our world more wonderful. For you. For me. For mankind. Because now, Wonderland Weather warmly welcomes our new colleagues from BROLLY."

Sir August removed his bear head and circled the table like the predator he was. "You all know who I am," he began, sounding positively avuncular. "And I know all of you. But you cannot know one another. Security is still paramount."

He moved round the table, pouring drinks and greeting each teddy personally while not using names. He seemed to be watching them closely for signs of discomfort or disloyalty. When he'd made the circuit, he stood again at the head of the table, paws clasped together in front of him. "Now, our organization faces its greatest test."

The shoulders of several of the teddies fell in dismay. The air was filled with tension as they awaited bad news. They didn't dare look at one another.

"I must demand absolute loyalty, absolute obedience." Sir August poured himself a drink, and took a sip while gazing at the assembled bears. He smacked his lips; they all knew he was partial to single-malt Scotch. "But anybody who wishes to resign must do so now. And in recognition of their work, a generous offer of one million pounds awaits them." He waited, looking round the table, a pleasant look on his face. The image of magnanimity itself.

"Now." Again, he surveyed the table, his hands extended in invitation. "Does anybody wish to leave?"

The teddies sneaked glances at each other through the eye slits in their masks, hesitant. No hands were raised.

"Please," Sir August said ingratiatingly, even kindly. "Don't be shy."

Up and down the table, the teddies sat quietly, still glancing furtively at each other. Meekly, one, then another, raised their hands.

Sir August focused on them as if they were the proverbial prodigal children. With kindness, he accepted their decision, and moved toward them as if to assure them of their continued acceptance. "Ah, yes. We owe so much. Both of you." Standing directly behind his assistants, he looked down at the backs of their teddy bear heads as they squirmed. "Without your work, my humble project would perish. How can I show my appreciation?"

Smiling beneficently, Sir August reached for the brooch holding the swath of tartan plaid over his shoulder, opened it and took out two tiny darts. As relaxed as if he were playing darts at the pub, he took one in each hand, and lightly pitched them into the necks of the teddies in front of him. They slumped onto the table, dead.

Sir August rubbed his hands together, and looked round the table. "Well. Any other business? No? Then, let us all be upstanding." He raised his glass, summoning the other teddies. They rose and lifted their glasses, but not one of them dared remove the teddy bear head to sip. Oblivious to their difficulty, Sir August spoke, looking sentimental.

"The toast is . . . to absent friends."

Steed and Emma looked left and right as they advanced down the corridor. There was no one about. They looked deceptively casual, but were in fact ready for anything. They advanced briskly toward a set of grand doors at the end of the hall. Each reaching for a door handle, they nodded at each other as they pulled open the doors in perfect unison.

A nearly deserted boardroom, with the exception of two teddies slumped at the table. Emma and Steed went to them quickly, Emma surveying the bear heads while Steed inspected the darts.

"Hmm . . . a bull's-eye," he said.

Emma leaned forward and picked up one of the teddy's heads, pulling the disguise off to reveal his face. "Alas, poor Babbington," she sighed. "I knew him well. Head of Prospero Research," she said, glancing at Steed. She lifted the mask off the other teddy. "And Morton, his assistant."

Steed shook his head. "To lose one scientist is a grave misfortune. To lose two . . ."

Noises in the corridor outside interrupted his eulogy for Babbington and Morton; Steed and Emma abandoned the dead teddies and dashed out the opposite door of the boardroom. Swiftly closing the door behind them, they surveyed the landscape of Wonderland Weather ahead. A corridor held two glass elevators, with a tangle of futuristic criss-crossing stairwells beyond.

Peering round a column, they saw a black teddy dart across to a stairwell and race upward, three steps at a time. A red teddy flew across the hallway and into a lift.

Steed leapt fiercely for the first elevator down, calling, "Follow that bear!"

Emma watched the door close on him, then raced down the corridor and up the stairs after the black teddy.

Steed, traveling down, looked across to the glass elevator opposite and saw a man-sized tartan teddy, traveling up, glaring at him. Steed, ever cool, ever calm, did a slow double-take and the teddy was gone—having been whisked upwards into the heights of the Wonderland Weather building.

Looking down through the glass of his descending elevator, Steed saw a truck being lowered on an automatic lift. Beside it sat a strange, cylindrical silver transmitter with a rounded top, bristling with antennae. Steed watched as the red teddy stepped out of his bear uniform. It was Bailey—Sir August's hired thug. Steed had seen him outside Trubshaw's in a black trench coat, and knew he was a hoodlum. Only hoodlums wore *black* trench coats. Not in the least surprised, he watched Bailey's minions load the sphere gently into the truck.

Steed stepped out of the elevator, swinging his umbrella, coming up behind the muscle boys loading the transmitter. The thugs wheeled at the gentle tapping of his leather-soled Trubshaw specials on the cement floor.

"I say," Steed said, as if he'd just come upon someone taking the last of the clotted cream.

The five men made a circle round him, eager to have a go at Steed.

Bailey, their leader, curled his upper lip. "A tailor's dummy. Look at that hat."

The men edged closer. Steed felt it was only fair to warn them.

"I wouldn't if I were you, lads," he said pleasantly.

"Well, I never," Bailey sniggered. "It talks."

With that, the smallest and most muscle-bound of the men took aim with his fist.

Steed ducked and Bailey took the punch. Wham! Steed coolly elbowed Bailey in the stomach, who, still reeling from his own man's punch, slumped against the wall.

Twisting, Steed kicked his preternaturally polished shoe into the gut of the man closest to him. The man gave a satisfying "Oooooof!" and Steed swiveled around to deliver a karate chop to first one throat, then another, of the three remaining bullies. Issuing impressive choking sounds, they soon slumped silently to the floor, looking a bit like sleeping children, Steed thought. *Bad* sleeping children.

"I say. Perfect timing," Steed commented as his bowler fell to earth, having been launched at some point in the scuffle. He caught it, and in one movement, wheeled round and smashed its steel brim into the face of the last goon. And Mrs. Peel questioned his choice of haberdashery. . . .

Steed surveyed the carnage around him: four thugs, varying from writhing to unconscious, on the floor. Bailey, having recovered from Steed's punch, half slid across the floor until he felt safe enough to stand and run to the truck. Steed, ever fastidious, dusted off and replaced his bowler, deciding that Bailey might be of more use to them at large than on the floor.

And he was right. Bailey, swearing a blue streak, madly punched a button to open the garage door to the outside while revving the engine of the truck. As he accelerated, from all appearances looking as if he were trying to drive out of hell itself, a paper flew out of his window. It was a paper that looked frightfully like a map, Steed thought, and snatched it as it floated to the floor.

"Tsk, tsk. Careless boy," he said, shaking his head as the squealing of Bailey's tires reached his ears from several streets away. He looked down at the map in his hand and smiled. At its center was a large X, with the words "WONDERLAND WEATHER TRANSMITTER" printed next to it in red ink.

CHAPTER ELEVEN

Hag-seed, hence!
The Tempest, *William Shakespeare*

Emma felt very much as if she were in a game of cat and mouse. She caught a glimpse of the black teddy climbing a staircase. But when she got to the foot of the stairs, she found a virtual maze of staircases flying off from it—some spiral, some straight, some up, some down.

A shadow darted across one of them somewhere above her, and she ran after it. As she came to the top of one staircase, she felt eyes on her again . . . but there was no one to be seen. Then she saw a shadow flitting beneath her, and she hurriedly descended a metal spiral staircase attached to the one she'd just climbed. The heels of her boots clattered down, until she heard—or rather *felt*—that there was someone above her. She looked but saw no one. Following instinct, she clam-

bered back up the spiral staircase, which she suspected
might lead to the stairs for the roof.

"Curiouser and curiouser," Emma panted, flying up
the stairs. She knew she was in luck when a door somewhere ahead and above her slammed violently. Racing
to the door, she grabbed the knob and pulled it open . . .
and found herself on the rooftop.

"Lovely view," she murmured, surveying the rooftops of Knightsbridge. Her head spun round as she
caught a flash of fake black fur in her peripheral vision.
Stalking like a cat, she furtively slunk between chimney
pots and air ventilator, next disappearing behind a row
of shrubbery as she followed the naughty teddy.

The rooftop was, she noticed, studded with minor
obstacles such as gables, a little fenced-in, shrubberied
garden for lunchtimes, Doric-looking pillars from some
beautification scheme that hadn't quite worked, and of
course, several rows of the inevitable blackened chimney pots.

Suddenly the bear darted out from behind the far
row of chimney pots. Emma pursued him, closing in,
saw him head toward the edge of the roof. A quick
glance after him revealed the maze of rooftops over
London, the same view one had from the Terrace Bar at
Harrods over tea, she thought.

Emma moved forward after the elusive bear, and
turned the corner round the last row of chimney pots.
She stopped short as she looked out over a dizzying
drop of several stories, directly to the street. Gasping,
feeling a touch of vertigo, she leaned backwards, then
put out her arms to right herself. For a moment she felt
she was hanging too far over the edge, and wouldn't be
able to recover.

At last she found her balance and her breath. Relieved to feel both her boot soles firmly on the roof,
she crouched, watching and listening for her prey. She

heard the mechanical-sounding flutter of a pigeon's wing . . . the wind whistling through the rooftop obstacles . . . then, from in front of her, a definite man-made noise.

Emma froze, every muscle tensed. *Another* noise. Her enemy was there. She suddenly saw a huge paw coming at her from behind a white pillar, then the entire beastly black teddy.

The blasted man in his absurd costume—what self-respecting villain would wear such a demeaning disguise, she wondered?—stood opposite Emma. Without hesitation he began to rain brutal blows on her with the heavy paws of the costume, seeing that his prey was virtually held captive. Emma was much too close to the edge of the roof—a mere eighteen inches, she thought—to fight effectively.

Unable to use her full array of fighting skills, aware that she might easily step backward over the edge, Emma concentrated on defensive tactics for the moment. She covered her head with already badly beaten arms, and struck out occasionally with a one-armed karate chop at the bear's torso.

But the heavy blows never let up long enough to allow her to counterattack. They came in a virtual hailstorm of force, each stunning strike driving home to her muscles and bones through her flesh. Despite all her skill, Emma found herself being beaten and bruised into a black leather heap. It was something of a surprise; she could honestly say that this was the first time she'd met her match in a fight. The sad fact was that her black belt in karate didn't count for much when her heels were a scant foot from disaster. And, as was proper in a fight, the bear wasn't giving any ground.

With the clarity of mind that comes in the midst of a life-threatening disaster, Emma felt a particularly brutal blow to her shoulder, with an accompanying explosion of pain. With grim certainty, she knew that the bear had dislocated it. It was one of her few physical weaknesses. The first dislocation had happened a decade ago, and she'd learned the hard way that once a shoulder is knocked out of its socket, it has more of a tendency to be displaced again.

Biting the inside of her cheek to manage the pain, Emma twisted the injured shoulder away from her attacker. Even as she did so, she knew she was revealing a weakness that he would capitalize upon. The excruciating pain made her go cold all over and slimy with sweat. Every movement intensified it cruelly. At least she didn't faint in these situations, Emma thought. She'd slogged through worse than this.

Through a growing fog of pain, as she did her best to ward off the incessant knockout-potential blows, she knew that the bear would interpret her first move of avoidance as a retreat. Emma knew it would move in for the kill soon.

And then it happened. Her ultimate dread became a reality. She'd known that any fighter worth his salt would advance, gaining ground rather than merely holding it. The bear took a step forward, and Emma took half a step backward in order not to be pushed over. The beating never relented for an instant, and it seemed to Emma that she was being pummeled by a machine. It was as if the animal was superhuman, indestructible, untiring. His succession of blows threw her off balance, and she reeled back, finally losing her balance completely.

She was certain that she would topple into space, flying silently through the air to Beauchamp Place below. Instead, *whooooomph!* Emma saw stars as the teddy thudded against her in a body blow that took them both down. When she hit the hard surface of the roof, her shoulder exploded in a flash of pain that was beyond bearing—even for her. To make matters worse, the wind was knocked out of her as she hung, suspended over the edge of the roof from the chest up, grappling with the murderous bear. He was not going to stop until he'd killed her, Emma knew.

She forced herself to fight with *both* hands against the bear's oppressive weight, gritting her teeth against the grating noises and unconscionable fiery blaze in her shoulder. Then the bear moved in for the last phase of the fight, its huge paws gripping her neck tightly, cutting off her air supply. Emma felt herself choking, saw stars again.

Extreme measures were called for. *I've been through worse than this*, Emma told herself, unwilling to surrender her life to such a ridiculous creature. Summoning all her reserves of energy and determination, she wrested her arms free, grinding her teeth as her shoulder was twisted cruelly once more, and mounted her attack. With her good arm, she delivered a devastating karate chop to the teddy's neck. She connected, and to her surprise, the bear's head flew up and off, revealing—

Herself. Emma gasped for breath, the bear having temporarily lost its hold on her neck. She sucked in great mouthfuls of air and gaped at her exact physical double.

"Well, well," Emma said when she had her breath back somewhat. Her voice sounded hard through the pain. "And who might you be?"

They stared at each other, stunned, locked in a lethal embrace. The bear had settled for pinning Emma to the roof now, hands brutally pressing down on her shoulders—no doubt in calculated cruelty—knees weighing heavily on her hips. Suddenly it dawned on Emma that *this* could be the woman in the photograph Mother had shown her! Something a bit different about the eyes, perhaps, but otherwise . . .

She's identical to me, Emma thought. *When I look in the mirror, that's who I see. Small wonder Mother and Steed thought I'd turned.* Except for those eyes . . . Cold. The bad Emma's eyes glinted like polished steel, eerily inhuman. And deadly.

Had Emma not been fighting for her life while suffering indescribable pain, she might have cheered. She wasn't a secret psychopath after all! Had she been able to move, she might have indulged in a small celebration.

Steed's shout startled them both. "Mrs. Peel!"

He flew from the stairs onto the roof, and stopped short as he saw the two Emmas together. Stunned, he moved toward them one disbelieving step at a time. Somewhere it clicked in Emma's mind that now she was safe; Steed had seen them together. Now *he* knew it hadn't necessarily been she in the Prospero security photo.

The bad Emma, evidently, wasn't about to be caught standing still. Emma gasped in pain as the woman released her with an all-too-intentional jolt to her shoulder. Her double leaped to her feet and catapulted off the roof in a jump of superhuman height, flying clear of the roof and seeming to hang in midair. They heard her land on a nearby rooftop somewhere below them, and the sound of running footsteps followed. Emma saw Steed's eyes flicking about in search of her, but Steed shook his head.

Steed, as matter-of-fact as if he were picking up his dry cleaning, pulled Emma up from the edge. Emma had been careful to hold out the hand of her good arm.

"Glad you happened by," she said breezily, dusting herself off. "Just in time to save me from myself." She shot him a curt little smile.

"I thought I was seeing double," Steed said.

"We both were," she said. Emma remembered her double's eyes with a shiver. She knew she could be frosty at times, but she hoped she was never as cold as that woman.

"By the way, I wonder if you might do me a small favor."

Steed made a little bow, looking surprised at her request. "At your service, Mrs. Peel."

She pointed to her shoulder, which hung at a disturbing angle, jutting forward out of her catsuit. She saw the horror on his face, saw his lips set in a grim line. So he knew about dislocated shoulders. "Would you be kind enough . . . ?"

He nodded brusquely and, to her infinite relief, firmly set his hands in exactly the right places to shift the wretched thing back into its socket. Clearly he'd done the dastardly deed once or twice before. He said, "Oh, look, the Queen's helicopter . . ." and as she glanced up, knowing that he was trying to distract her, he did it. Bone ground on bone as he jerked and shifted the shoulder back into position.

She closed her eyes and bit the inside of her lip, tasting blood. A cold sweat covered her body as she composed herself in silence, standing rigidly on the rooftop. Somehow she knew that he had averted his eyes respectfully. When she opened her eyes, he was casting a glance over the rooftops for the runaway double.

"Ready to shoulder—I mean soldier—on?" he asked, finally turning to meet her eyes.

"Indeed, Steed," she said, and walked ahead of him toward the stairway off the roof.

Bad Emma landed, furious, on the roof of the most famous department store in the world. She stripped off the heavy teddy bear suit, relieved to be back in black leather again. How she hated that suit! Though she'd do anything for *him*, and he'd insisted. Just as he'd insisted that she bring Emma Peel in alive. Well, she was smart enough to know when it was necessary to disobey. And if she ever wanted Sir August, she'd have to kill Emma Peel.

Fuming, she strode to a structure on the roof containing a doorway that was likely to house stairs down into the store. She'd had the perfect opportunity to kill the Peel woman, and she'd so nearly done it! The woman's face was going a satisfying shade of purple when she'd somehow managed that disastrous karate chop. And she'd had her at such a disadvantage, too, at the very edge of the roof. To make matters worse, the woman had seen her face. Damn!

She'd have to ask Sir August to install some better swear words in her lexicon, she thought, opening the door into a scented room full of women's evening clothes. He hadn't given her many. He'd said something to the effect of that being all she needed. But she did need more. Many, many more.

Perhaps getting rid of Emma Peel was going to be more difficult than she thought. She ignored the admiring eyes of the shoppers, mostly cheerful, overweight Americans and swarthy Middle Easterners, and disregarded the saleswoman's offer of help. She knew she looked good, with her firm muscles and long, lean body, but what did it all matter if there was another body just like hers? With a superior brain?

Bad Emma clenched her teeth and rode the escalators down, floor after floor. No doubt she'd get another chance at Mrs. Emma Peel. There were others who wanted the woman dead, after all. She arrived at the ground floor, feeling a bit better. Her eyes were drawn to a counter displaying bottles of bright red nail polish. That's it, she thought. I'll work harder to make myself a suitable replacement for Mrs. Peel.

She set off toward the counter with grim determination, a nasty smile creeping up one side of her mouth.

• • •

Bailey was hard at work with his power screwdriver when Sir August surprised him, appearing at his side in the lab in his teddy outfit. He had to admit, as bizarre as the teddy bear disguises had seemed at first, the black furry outfit with the tartan accents did fit his deranged master. Looking down at his own red fur, Bailey thought that he could endure far worse for the opportunity to be so cruel to so many people for Sir August. And the teddy bear head did nicely mask his identity. . . .

"We need time to prepare," Sir August said. "They're getting too close, too soon." He bent over the lab table where Bailey had assembled the parts of Sir August's latest attack mechanism. "Let's look at you, my little darlings." He watched Sir August fondle the bizarre bits of the machines he was assembling, the metallic legs, rotor wings, and camera-lens eyes of giant mechanical attack bees. Bailey turned back to his task, buzzing with the power screwdriver as he mounted the left gun in one of the nearly finished bees' mouths.

"I hope Teddy's been treating you nicely," Sir August said indulgently to his inanimate little pets, running his hand over the rear of the bee, where the stinger would normally be.

"Unleash the bees!" he shouted, and Bailey obliged, pressing a button on a remote control next to him. Sir August yanked his hand back just as a foot-long silver stiletto shaft popped up from the bee's backside, quivering like a dart.

"Let's see how they like a little sting in their tail." He laughed like the maniac Bailey knew him to be, the maniac for whom he loved to kill and maim. Sir August's laugh echoed through the lab, crescendoing as sound reverberated endlessly off the stainless steel walls. Soon the room was filled with the sound of a million maniacs, all overcome with mad hilarity, as the laughter broke into weird shafts of sound that shot back at them from all angles.

Bailey smiled. This job really did have its merits.

CHAPTER TWELVE

A plague upon this howling! They are louder than the weather or our office.

The Tempest, *William Shakespeare*

It was the temporary headquarters from heaven. Who ever would have guessed that Ministry mucky-mucks and operatives were barreling about London in the dark aboard a red double-decker bus? And the safe cover was only one of its advantages. It was exceptionally convenient transportation, and no one could hear Mother and Father bickering over the cacophony of London traffic.

Steed sat with the others upstairs, listening to Mother attempt to regain control of the debriefing. Father had become more and more feisty of late, Steed thought. He wondered for the hundredth time if she really was blind or if she merely used her supposed handicap to gain an advantage when she needed it most.

"So now you're saying there are *two* Mrs. Peels?" Mother sounded distinctly skeptical.

Father harrumphed. "How preposterous."

"Let *me* handle this, Father. I'm in charge—"

"So you keep saying," Father said wryly.

Steed unfurled his newspaper as Mother and Father began to bicker like a married couple. Normally he found it comical, but he'd had enough of it just recently.

"*You never* consider my point of view," Father shouted. "It's as if I simply don't exist. And who made you head of this Ministry?"

Mother huffed, raising his voice in return. "Good Lord, woman, you *always* forget that I'm not doing this for my own enjoyment. Do you think I *like* . . . ?"

On and on they went as the bus careered through London in the night.

Mother spat, "You made your point about Mrs. Peel, very succinctly—"

"We both know who's responsible. This whole story's a red herring. Quite impossible . . ." Father rejoined.

Mother held up a finger that would have been extremely irritating to Father, had she been able to see it. "Ah-ah-ah: nothing's impossible, Father. I often think of at least six impossible things before breakfast."

An embarrassed silence reigned, which only served to reinforce exactly what impossible things Mother dreamed of in those early morning hours. Half listening, since he'd heard Mrs. Peel's name mentioned, Steed took note. He'd always wondered how far Mother's disability extended. . . .

"Thank you for your contribution, Father," Mother said, recovering. "If you'll kindly allow me to continue—Steed? As you were saying . . ."

Steed looked up from the paper. "Oh. Have you finished?" He smiled. "Someone's recruiting your Prospero scientists into a cover organization. But *not* Mrs. Peel."

Mother tried to preempt Father's inevitable question

by asking it himself. "If you're so sure she's innocent, do you have another suspect?"

Steed chewed his lip. "I may. What makes you so sure of an attack?"

Mother sighed. "The World Council of Ministers meets on Saint Swithin's Day. Patron saint of—"

"Weather," Father said grimly. "You see?"

"That's what I've been trying to tell you." Had it not been for the cruel torture he and every other boy had received at the hands of the upper-form boys at public school, Steed wouldn't have had the self-control to refrain from shaking them both by their starched collars. "I saw *both* Mrs. Peels. With my own eyes."

Father simply could not resist the final word. It was in her nature. "Personally, I've always thought eyes were much overrated."

"We can't waste any more time," Mother said, exasperated. He pressed the bell; the bus pulled to the curb and stopped. "He has his orders." Mother turned to Steed. "Clock's ticking, Steed. I'm counting on you."

Steed saw the lay of the land. Mother or Father was going to win this battle, and it was quite possibly for keeps. He nodded to Mother. "Cheerio, then."

He descended the stairs of the bus, glad to escape from the caustic atmosphere on the upper deck. He saw, looking out the windscreen, that the bus was stopping outside Mrs. Peel's flat. Heading for the exit, Steed passed Brenda, Mother's bodyguard, this time dressed as a bus conductor.

"My stop," he said, doffing his hat to her. "Keep the change."

Brenda smiled encouragingly at John before he hopped off the bus. Then she blushed, feeling the heat all the way down to her chest, in the afterglow of his attention. Tears came to her eyes at the thought of his nobility.

He was risking his life, moving in on the dangerous psychopath Sir August de Wynter, yet he was able to make witty jokes with her—practically as he walked to his doom.

She could hear Mother and Father arguing above, and knew that time was growing short. Mother had taken her aside and told her to be on the alert; Father was up to something sinister. Sooner or later there would be a showdown, he had said, and they—Mother and Brenda—would have to be ready.

Brenda patted the switchblade safely stowed down her bra, sheathed in white leather. Given Mother's condition, her duty as bodyguard became all the more important. Should Father threaten him physically, which she found difficult to imagine, she would be ready. *And God forbid that John should be caught in the cross fire,* she thought. She wasn't about to let that happen. She'd fight to the death. . . .

Lost in thought, she went to sit behind the driver. She wondered if John knew she had been trained by the Ministry in physical defense—that she was actually something of an athlete. Ministry employees were forbidden to know one another socially, and in a way that was more than acceptable to her.

She looked down at her hands, which bore no rings. She was saving herself for him, would be devoted to him no matter what. Even if he chose this Mrs. Peel over her, though she was quite certain that was a passing fancy, Brenda would be there waiting when the dust settled. If she spent the next forty years watching him, being the helping hands supporting him at the office, that would be enough for her. Merely to be associated with such a man was educational.

John Steed had, in fact, made her career more worthwhile. There were times when, in her duties, she had saved his life. She had successfully obtained weapons and other equipment for him. She'd also noticed in the case reports she'd typed—studying his meticulous jottings all the while—that occasionally those items had allowed him to prevail.

When John received his K.B.E., thenceforth Sir John, she would be there in the background, silently cheering him on. She wanted nothing more from life.

Inside Emma's flat, the clock ticked and the kettle hissed, punctuating the civilized silence of a game of chess. Steed and Emma sat at opposite sides of the chessboard, surrounded by crumpled weather charts on the floor. The BROLLY map, revealing the site of the transmitter, sat among them. Emma studied the charts, not the chessboard, nibbling a chocolate finger.

Steed pretended to study the board, but found it difficult to tear his eyes away from the shiny, satin strapless orange dress she wore. Not so much the dress, actually, but her shoulders, and, well, upper chest. When he'd arrived, fresh off the bus, she claimed to have just returned from the theatre.

"Mother and Father are convinced an attack will take place," Steed said. "Could someone like Sir August really target a kind of weather bomb?" He thought for a moment, considering the board. "Knight to rook four."

"Certainly," Emma replied. "If they knew what they were doing. Imagine this . . ." She held up a chocolate finger in one hand. He tried hard to focus on the hand, instead of where his eyes longed to go. ". . . Is a radio signal, and this"—she pointed to her mouth—"is the transmitter. It's merely a question of "—the biscuit floated toward her open mouth—"hitting the right target. Then—boom!!" She bit into it with ferocity.

Glancing briefly at the chessboard, she said, "Queen to knight three. Check." She sighed in a way that made Steed's heart leap unhealthily, and pointed back at the map. "Look. I've been charting these weather outbreaks. Are you paying attention?" Emma picked up a pointer from next to her chair and swished it over the maps like a schoolmistress with an authority complex.

"Absolutely," Steed said. It was all too much to take. He labored to keep his face devoid of expression as he surveyed her stick, then willed his eyes to return to her face. "And I'm a believer in firm discipline."

"Do you always obey orders?" Emma gave him a stern look, tapping the pointer impatiently on the papers.

"Always. Except . . . when I don't. Knight to bishop four." He took a moment to move the piece and take hers; she was black, he was white. Quite appropriate, under the circumstances, he thought, considering the temptation she represented—not to mention what Father thought of her.

"For example," Steed continued slowly, staring with discipline at the chequered board. "If I were, perish the thought, under orders to kill you . . ."

"Pity you never told me," Emma said, now slapping the pointer against the palm of her open hand. He was trying to keep his eyes on the chessboard but had caught a glimpse of her shoulders above that dress. He couldn't get the sight of her on the rooftop, her shoulder hanging horribly out of place beneath the black leather, out of his mind. She had been far more brave than he would have been under the circumstances. The number of times that had happened to him, and he'd actually cried out . . . but she was looking at him now. Better say something.

"Never asked, did you?" he said nonchalantly. "Can't mention everything, after all. And we were getting on so well."

"You didn't want to spoil the fun."

"It would have put a damper on things, don't you agree?"

"I'm intrigued. Queen to bishop six." She moved the

piece, the smooth curve of the muscles in her arm distracting him. "What did you have in mind? Nothing too messy, I hope."

Steed pulled his eyes away from her creamy arm and shot her a look of reprimand. "Now, Mrs. Peel. There's no need to dwell on the unsavory aspects. After all, according to your file you're a psychopathic personality with schizophrenic delusions suffering from recurring amnesia based on traumatic repression leading to outbursts of antisocial and violent behavior." He paused. "Knight to bishop four. Check."

Steed moved his piece, allowed his words to sink in. For a moment he regretted it; she actually looked rather hurt. Beautiful, but hurt. Still, he'd decided to tell her what Father thought, and tell her he had. She would soon realize that the very fact he'd done so proved he was on *her* side.

"Is that really what you think of me?" Her voice was clear and hard.

"Oh, well," Steed responded. "Just my type, Mrs. Peel." He wondered if she guessed how true those words were.

"Good. Because I think I've found something."

"You never fail to surprise me," he said. It was true.

Emma pointed to the BROLLY map. "On this map. A cluster of microclimates round a single area. Very strange."

Steed leaned over to see what she meant. The light green circles to which she pointed clustered around the X labeled as the site of the Wonderland Weather transmitter.

"Hmm. X marks the spot, eh? Your move, Mrs. Peel."

Emma reached over to move her piece on the chessboard. Steed averted his eyes from her, focusing instead on the board. "Queen takes knight. Checkmate."

And she had won indeed, Steed thought, if she could prove the existence of the weather plot *and* Bad Emma.

He was much relieved now that he knew Mrs. Peel hadn't shot him. And, though he'd been humiliated once again, this time over a chessboard, he had to give her credit. She was a champion at chess as well.

Bad Emma. Yes, he liked that name for the double. But he strongly suspected Good Emma could be a bit naughty herself in certain respects. He only hoped he'd get the chance to find out.

Gad! The old bat even cheated at croquet, Sir August thought as her mallet thudded dully against the ball. It was disgusting. He and Father were playing in the Hallucinogen Hall grounds, near the lake. Emerald-green grass surrounded them, perfectly watered by Wonderland Weather's "Turf Tender" package. He took great pride in his croquet grounds. Yet here they were, on *his* home turf, and there was *her* ball, mysteriously curving toward the hoop. As if magnetically drawn . . .

And she was *blind*!

"I can't hold off the Ministry much longer. This Mrs. Peel, I'm warning you—don't let her get too close." Despite her blindness, Father seemed to know that her ball had passed cleanly, miraculously, through the hoop. Sir August saw from her expression that she was contemplating victory. It made him sick.

"Good shot," he muttered, through clenched teeth. *Mutton dressed as lamb,* he told himself. "Haven't I always taken care of you? We are partners, after all. Even though we've never seen eye to eye." A bit cruel, he supposed, but irresistible. She was a tough old trout, anyway.

"Why not leave Mrs. Peel to me?"

"Don't worry," Sir August said. "I'll take care of her." If only he could, he thought. He stood on Father's ball, treading it into the ground. "You're playing rather well. Shall we double the bet?"

Father hit her ball up in the air, missing the hoop for once.

"Oh dear. Tough luck. Just missed. I win, again." He wondered if the falseness even came through to her, treacherous as she was herself.

"I'm not sure you appreciate the danger. They do say love is blind."

"That would make two of us," Sir August muttered to himself as he banged her ball away toward a steep bank. "I think you'll stand a better chance starting over there," he said loudly, trying to sound kind. He set her off toward the edge of the cliff, while he himself walked on toward his ball.

There was a loud, satisfying crash from the direction of the bank. Sir August turned, a gleam in his eye.

"Mind how you go."

CHAPTER THIRTEEN

How lush and lusty the grass looks! How green!
The Tempest, *William Shakespeare*

The screeching tires of Emma's Jaguar sent birds flapping, alarmed, from their green perches deep in the English countryside. The Jaguar clung to the tarmac as she rounded a sharp curve on the narrow road at top speed, then flew over a humpback bridge and somehow managed to stay on four wheels round successive bends. She went round a blind corner without the merest tap of the brake pedal, and shot forward into the straight road ahead, flooring the accelerator.

Steed didn't mind the way Emma deliberately accelerated the Jaguar when she saw the "SLOW: BENDS" sign. He didn't even mind her racing round the blind corners, utterly without regard for his life. She obviously had a death wish, the way she was driving. She had even dressed for action—and possibly death—in the black leather catsuit again. Probably something to do with the husband . . . yes, he'd have to get round to all that at some point.

He was hanging on with white knuckles when she glanced over, smiling. He relaxed his hands by his sides, on the seat, embarrassed to have been caught out.

"I thought you lived on the edge, Mrs. Peel. Is this as fast as you can go?"

"Have I trespassed on a male prerogative, Mr. Steed?" She glanced in the rearview mirror. "We're being followed."

Steed heard a strange buzzing sound and turned to look out the rear window as Emma checked in the mirror. "What's that noise?" he asked, cocking his head in perplexity as he tried to make it out. The Jaguar zoomed down the country lane as, in confusion, Steed perceived what appeared to be—but surely *couldn't* be—a swarm of giant bees approaching from the rear. There were perhaps a dozen or more, now advancing until they flew directly over the car. They began to swoop down upon them, firing guns and dropping small but deadly bombs that fortunately missed the Jaguar—so far.

Steed stuck his head out the window in disbelief, noting that these bees were not your usual garden variety. These were giant mechanical bees, sporting rotors for loft and what appeared to be guns for mouths, like jet fighters. The buzzing was deafening. Steed shouted in Emma's ear, "Insects. Bigger every year . . ." He shook his head regretfully. Well, he knew how to handle bees.

Shots blasted into the roof of the Jag. They were under attack.

"Hold on!" Emma shouted, and slammed her foot down. The car reached speeds of which Steed wouldn't have believed it was capable. His head was pinned back against the seat. *I shouldn't wonder we're pulling Gs,* he thought. He could see Emma's hair tossing wildly in the wind.

Great Goodyears, but she was gorgeous.

"Here we go," she yelled gleefully, and pumped the accelerator.

Steed's eyes widened, and with difficulty he reached a hand atop his bowler and clamped it firmly down on his head. The Jaguar twisted and turned on the single-track lanes, Emma driving expertly as the shots ricocheted off the roof. Cannons seemed to blast the car—these bees were extraordinarily unfriendly, Steed thought. He glanced at Emma, who drove calmly, a grim little smile on her face. Was there *anything* she couldn't do? He would begin to feel seriously inadequate, and quite soon, if this went on.

Ripping his eyes from Emma and looking back to the road, Steed saw bullets tearing up the tarmac ahead of them, forcing Emma to turn the Jag in wild evasive maneuvers. The rotors and engines of the giant insects roared as they pursued the car from the sky, firing their huge, powerful guns and dropping their little bombs, barely missing the car as Emma piloted it through tortuous twists and turns. A bomb burst on the port side, blasting the car sideways. Still, the Jaguar held the road. Remarkable, these British motors, Steed thought.

In the next moment he realized that Emma had gained a small advantage over the bees; their deafening drone had receded slightly. The countryside flew by. Emma raced past a crossroads, snaked round a hairpin curve, and came into a long, gradual bend. She pushed her foot to the floor, and Steed felt himself thrown back against the seat. Just what modifications had she made to this thing? The pilot, he thought . . . the husband pilot had no doubt heavily modified the motor and stuffed the engine compartment with twin superchargers, water injection, and who knew what else. She probably thought of him when she drove it. . . .

Checking through the rear window, Steed saw that the beasts had indeed fallen behind. Turning back to the

road, he saw that the merry chase was approaching a
very narrow, very low railway bridge with appalling
speed. It loomed before them ominously, appearing to
be roughly the height of the opening in a Buckingham
Palace guardhouse, and roughly the same width. *Never
make it at this speed,* Steed thought, wincing. Nevertheless, Emma gunned the motor and drove the car straight
through.

In the next moment Steed heard a resounding *crash!*
soon followed by a *kaboom!* Swiveling to look out the
back window, he saw that several of the bees had
smashed into the bridge and exploded. Flames shot
from their metallic hulls as huge, charred metal bee legs
and dismembered rotor wings tumbled to the tarmac.

Emma revved the motor and emerged on the other
side of the bridge with several fewer bees on her tail. But
the others were still in hot pursuit and seemed to be gaining ground. *Pesky things,* Steed thought. Gazing through
the rear window, he saw the bees zeroing in with determination. One nasty-looking unnatural insect seemed to be
accelerating faster than the others toward them.

Steed suddenly felt Emma brake as she attempted to
take the car through a sharp, right-angle corner at an
ungainly speed. But while the Jag slowed, Steed realized
in a flash that the bee wouldn't. Flinching, he shouted a
warning to Emma before closing his eyes and covering
his face with one arm. Glass exploded into the car from
the rear window, and the giant bee's guns continued to
fire directly through the windscreen. The insect was
stuck in the back seat, and Steed saw that it would continue to fire away until he swatted it into submission.
Perhaps he could make use of those guns. . . .

Steed grabbed his umbrella from the floor and, grimacing at his all-too-clear view of the beast's ugly visage, stabbed its sharp tip into each of the eyes in turn,
noting that the eye holes housed twin video camera

lenses. So they were being monitored. . . . Emma pushed
her foot down again without a word, looking as if she
were rather enjoying herself. Steed went to work on
the twin guns that were mounted in what might have
been an ordinary bee's mouth. If he could just dismantle
them . . .

He flipped open the screwdriver compartment on his
umbrella handle and activated the power switch, removing the screws that held the guns in place even as they
spewed bullets that whistled through the car. As Steed
got the first gun to fall from the bee, he felt the car jerk
backward from the blast of a bomb. Peering through the
windscreen, he saw that it had blasted a rather impressive hole in the ground directly in front of them. Emma
was forced to turn the Jaguar onto a wooded track, and
they bounced and jostled along as Steed made his best
effort to unscrew the second gun. At last it dropped, and
he threw the first one into Emma's lap before beginning to fire up at the attacking bees overhead through
his window. They continued to fire down on him at
the same time, their bullets whizzing past the edges of
his hat.

Even as he focused on eliminating the insects overhead, Steed admired Emma's brave effort to dodge the
trees in the wood while shaking their attackers. The
bees followed, homing in on them even in the dense
wood, until *splattt!* Two bees simultaneously smashed
into beech trees and exploded.

With two fewer bees on their tail, the count was now
down to five. *Much more manageable,* Steed thought.
He fired from the rear window at the approaching dive
bombers, startled to see a black Mini parked at the side
of the track. *Blast,* he thought. Mechanical bees were
ever so much simpler than humans.

Steed focused now on the Mini as much as the bees,
noting with alarm that the Mini was somehow advancing

on them. How could that measly insect of a car possibly approach the powerful Jaguar?

Zinggg! A bullet whipped through the car next to Steed as he returned fire. *Whizzz!* He ducked as another, and yet another bullet narrowly missed him. Nipping up for another quick volley of shots, he could just make out that nasty Bailey bloke behind the wheel, along with his mate Donovan. Donovan was firing straight at them. Suddenly a fusillade of bullets came from above, and Steed had to duck and inch forward into the dash to avoid them. Crouching on the floor of the Jaguar, Steed returned fire on the bee, and saw to his satisfaction that he'd hit the thing bang on. The bee began to spin to the ground, looking very much like a failing airplane at an air show, its rotors spinning as it plummeted to the floor of the wood.

Steed glanced at his human attackers and saw Bailey lifting his gun to fire. But he also saw Bailey's face register the shock of the bee crashing into the Mini's path, obstructing them as it spun and fired blindly.

Donovan took evasive action, swerving to avoid the bee, which continued to fire into the Mini. Bullets exploded off the little car, pinging and ricocheting. Steed looked out of the rear window as Donovan attempted to control the vehicle, crashing into the forest through saplings and underbrush.

Emma piloted the Jaguar on through the forest as Steed watched the bees disperse, spinning out of control in all directions. As he watched, another one slammed into a tree trunk and met its end. *The beekeeper is undone,* he thought, smiling. It was over. He let out a laugh and smiled at Emma, who began to drive a straight course through the wood.

But then Steed heard something behind them and wheeled in his seat. Donovan and Bailey came crashing out of the woods in the now considerably rumpled Mini, onto the track behind them. Steed saw the bees flying in formation above and behind them, falling back in behind the Jaguar. "Damn! They're back on our tail!"

A sudden clamor on the roof made Steed look up. With an instinctive awareness of imminent attack, Steed fired through the roof as a long, razor-sharp stiletto blade shot through the roof of the car, sliding into the space just next to his right ear. With a look of strong disapproval, Steed realized that the bees were, of course, equipped with stingers. Why hadn't he anticipated this?

A second bee suddenly appeared, clinging to the roof with apparently magnetic feet while trying to climb in through the windscreen. Steed shot it, redirected his aim to the bee on the roof, and fired again. He saw movement on the windscreen and turned to see bees swarming all over the front of the car, climbing atop one another in an unseemly bee frenzy. Emma accelerated, turned the wheel, swerving the Jag from one side of the track to the other, smashing the bees against trees and fence posts. Steed saw her actually grin as two of the oversized insects fell away, crumpled, then two more fell dismembered from the car.

Only one remained now, on the rear of the car, near the petrol filler cap. Steed aimed his gun at it, but saw that it had already fired its stinger, puncturing the petrol tank. Fuel leaked out onto the dirt track behind them in a steady stream. Steed shot anyway, dislodging the bee from its spot over the tank. The bee lost its grip and crashed into the petrol trail, igniting it and creating a respectable bonfire as the flame spread along the path as if traveling along a wick.

With satisfaction, Steed turned back to look ahead through the windscreen just in time to see a rogue bee flying straight toward them, shooting up the dirt track just ahead of the car. Emma shifted gears and accelerated, making straight for it. Steed glanced at her, in awe of the grim determination he saw in her face. *This is it*, he thought. *Been nice knowing you, Mrs. Peel.*

But the bee hit the Jag's bonnet squarely and careered through the air, somersaulting over the roof. Steed noticed, openmouthed, that it was hurtling straight for Donovan and Bailey in the Mini. It landed squarely in the center of their windscreen, smashing through it. Steed felt the Jag swerve severely to one side, nearly overturning, and looked out the window. Awestruck, he saw that Emma had only just avoided flying off a steep escarpment that would have plunged them to almost certain death.

Steed wheeled again in his seat to watch the Mini negotiate the turn, and saw the horror-stricken faces of the men inside as they flew into the abyss. The Mini bounced on its nose, then rolled. As Emma continued to pilot the Jaguar forward through the wood, revving the motor, Steed caught a glimpse of Bailey and Donovan emerging from the crumpled Mini. The two men were fighting their way up the steep bank, through the brush toward the track.

Emma accelerated. Steed heard the reassuring roar of the motor, but felt a niggling discomfort as he saw petrol slosh out into the road behind them. Not good, that. She rounded a curve at high speed, skidding as she went, putting good distance between them and the two attackers. Steed turned to the front again just in time to see a horrific sight: a little old lady stood bang in the middle of the road, directly in their path. Emma grimaced and braked heavily, the Jag screeching to a halt half an inch from the woman.

Steed climbed out of the car with Emma, concerned, just as Bailey and Donovan emerged from the deep gully with their guns trained on them. Stunned, Steed gaped at the septuagenarian as she said sweetly, "Would you please be so kind as to hit the ground—if it's not too much trouble?"

Steed recognized the woman as Alice, Dr. Darling's

pram-pushing knife-thrower and Mother's favorite—one of the Ministry faithfuls he'd always trusted. He wasn't fooled by the sweetly flowered Liberty cotton dress, covered by a hand-knit gray cardigan that matched her severe gray bun. Her eyes twinkled from beneath crepey, wrinkled lids. Steed saw Emma's jaw drop as the woman produced a tommy gun and promptly sprayed bullets into Donovan, who crumpled, his gun spinning along the road. Bailey ran for his life as Steed and Emma turned to look at their unlikely rescuer.

"I do hope he was a baddy. . . ." she said thoughtfully, staring at Donovan's body for a moment before turning to Emma. "My name's Alice. Mother said you'd be on your way. You must be Mrs. Peel."

It wouldn't do to omit introductions, Steed thought. Where were his manners?

"Mrs. Peel? Alice . . ."

Emma smiled and bowed her head. "How d'you do?"

There was a rustling sound as Donovan, mortally wounded but still alive, reached with outstretched fingers for his gun. Alice wheeled, delivering two more bullets right between his eyes. He was utterly, incontrovertibly, dead, Steed noted. Alice always did a most thorough job.

"Poor boy," she said under her breath. Turning to Steed, she asked, "You with Mother or Father?"

"Both, actually."

"Glad to see they're together at last. They don't get along. Promotion . . . top job . . . most unfair. Quite a fuss at the Ministry."

Steed wasn't concentrating. Office gossip had never been of interest to him. As far as he was concerned, there was no place for petty skirmishes and personal vendettas in the Ministry. "You don't say," he said absently. They began to walk toward the car, and Steed thought he heard a crackling sound, but couldn't place it. He cast a glance around the wood, distracted, but saw nothing.

"Someone didn't want you to get to the party," Alice said.

"I expect we'll have to gate-crash," Emma said.

Alice chuckled. "I may be able to help. This way . . ."

Kaboom! Steed found himself on the pavement, feeling blasted and scorched. The petrol tank. Of course—they'd left a trail of the stuff for the flames to follow. He gazed at the flaming wreck that had once been Emma's Jaguar. A shame, really. Emma shrugged as they picked themselves up and dusted off. Alice led the way up the road. Up ahead they saw the wall-like battlements of Hallucinogen Hall, with the "No Trespassers" sign Steed knew so well. He pulled out the BROLLY map and studied it.

"Excuse me," Alice said, pausing. "You *are* a Gemini, Mrs. Peel?"

Emma smiled. "How did you guess?"

Steed looked up from his map in time to see that Alice looked as if Emma had just said something very significant. *Never knew she was into all that astrology rot,* he thought, grimacing.

He looked at the Hall ahead, then referred again to his map. "There's Wonderland Weather. Spot on." They couldn't help but notice that all around them it was a murky, cloudy, all-too-English day. But the sun shone brightly over the Hall in eerie splendor.

On the perfect green lawn of the Hall, a mechanical peacock flared its tail, whirring ever so discreetly as its camera recorded images of Alice, Steed and Emma inside the walls.

Emma never saw it. She was too busy following Alice, who was stealthily crossing the open lawn to the cover of a substantial-looking maze, not far away. Emma had to laugh to herself. But for the skulking about, they would look like a family group out for a Sunday stroll: the kindly grandmother, still on her top form; the well-dressed, well-mannered gentleman; and the devoted wife—though devoted to exactly whom remained to be seen.

Alice led in her sensible brogues, motioning for them to follow as she entered the maze. "Along here," she said quietly. The three continued down the slate path within the hedges, surrounded by perfectly maintained six-foot-tall boxwood. Its fresh scent was momentarily deceiving to Emma; it made her feel she was at her leisure in the maze of her childhood home. Ah, now *that* had been a maze . . .

After turning several corners, they came to a curve. "Most innovative design," Steed said, intrigued. "Curves in a maze . . ."

"And slopes," Emma said. "Quite unusual."

Alice slipped behind as they traveled through the maze. "Look! It's a lesser spotted bunting!" she said, pulling tiny binoculars from her handbag, hanging back to view the specimen.

Steed paused momentarily at a bank of roses that sheltered in a corner, perfectly manicured and utterly without ladybirds. He plucked off one of the blooms. "On behalf of the Flower Lovers of Ross and Cromarty Association, I would like to present this to you, Mrs. Peel—'The Perfect Englishwoman.' "

Emma turned slowly to look at him, unsure of his meaning. It was unlike him to . . . then she saw the rose. He had plucked a tall, cool white rose with dew on its petals and was holding it out to her.

"Mind the thorns," he said, and walked on as she paused to take it.

Shaking her head, she raced head of him, throwing the rose down in his path. "There is no perfect Englishwoman," she tossed over her shoulder. "Or didn't you know?"

"Ah! I've found a weakness. Not much on horticulture, are you? You'd best check your *Guide to British Roses*, Mrs. Peel," Steed reprimanded. She heard his pace increase to keep up with her as she strode ahead. "Ivory color, perfectly shaped petals, distinctive scent, developed by an Englishman."

She could have crawled under the slate of the path to join the pillow bugs. Fortunately, her knowledge of mazes saved the day. "Aha . . . Yes . . . It's clear now. A love maze in a trapezoidal shape, originally a late seventeenth-century design, then copied."

Emma slipped round the next corner, relieved to have extricated herself from Steed. If he weren't so damnably attractive, and clever, and unflappable . . . She heard Steed coming after her, looked back as he caught a glimpse of her. Soon she heard him on the opposite side of the hedge.

"Over here," she said. "By your side."

She was so perverse, she told herself. One moment she threw roses back at his feet, the next she was practically making declarations of love. *Oh well*, she sighed. *A woman's prerogative.*

"I was worried," he said from behind the hedge, tongue in cheek.

Emma saw a propitiously placed hole in the wall of green boxwood where some bird had once nested. She stuck her face through and nearly surprised Steed. "How touching. Afraid you'd lost me?"

"No. That you might escape," he said with icy calm.

She wondered if there were a rose called Blushing Berk; it would suit her perfectly now. How *did* he feel about her, blast him? Perhaps he was as confused as she was.

"Still suspicious, I see." She hoped her tone didn't reveal too much.

"Just wondering if you brought me here under false pretenses."

Humor was the best antidote. "Frankly, I'm *amazed* that you would think such a thing." She kept moving. This verbal parrying was growing old. "Perhaps I should run away."

"I'll have to give chase," he said, matter-of-factly.

She gritted her teeth. Part of her longed for him to do just that. "I'll hide. How romantic. Do try. . . ."

She ducked and ran silently, deeper into the maze. She knew its design; she would lose him. Pausing for a moment, she heard him say, "Ah! There you are, Mrs. Peel," but in the wrong direction. Frowning, she wondered if he'd lost his senses completely as she heard him run off the way they'd come, away from her. Wait a moment; were there . . . yes, *two* sets of footsteps.

She heard something behind her and swiveled round, poised to attack. She did a rapid double-take. It was her evil twin, Bad Emma, dressed in an identical black leather catsuit. *How, in the name of all that was British, did she know what I was wearing?* Emma wondered. They looked each other up and down, then Bad Emma disappeared around the corner.

Emma gave chase, following close behind. She rounded corners close on the heels of the woman, but always seemed to be just a bit too far behind. Emma increased her speed, trying to catch up, but at one point she zigged when she should have zagged, and got going down the wrong path. If she hadn't known the maze design, it was doubtful she would have recovered from that mistake.

At last she had Bad Emma in sight again, and was gaining on her rapidly. Racing over a patch of path strewn with leaves, she felt the ground give way beneath her. She wasn't at all the screaming sort, but she came close to caterwauling as she fell down, down, through a vertical tunnel of seemingly endless depth. Tumbling through the darkness, she reached out to check her fall, but was spinning too fast, bouncing from one side of the wall to the other.

Corkscrewing head over heels downward, ricocheting from side to side of the tunnel, she just had time to think, *Alice in bloody Wonderland* . . . before there was only blackness.

CHAPTER FOURTEEN

How now? moody? What is't thou canst demand?
                    The Tempest, *William Shakespeare*

Steed rounded yet another corner in the maddening maze and saw Emma far away, down a rare straight stretch. She disappeared again, and he pursued her, actually becoming a bit irritated with her game-playing as he reached the end of the long stretch and rounded . . .

Wham! A silver staff flew down in front of him, blocking his path. As he recovered his balance, he found himself face to face with . . .

"Sir August de Wynter," the madman said.

Steed followed suit and introduced himself. So few people had proper manners these days. . . .

"John Steed."

As if to illustrate Sir August's strength, the silver staff flew back and forth, up and down in front of Steed with blinding speed, spinning and blurring as Sir August almost magically wielded his weapon.

"An old trick I learned from a dervish in Istanbul." Sir August had barely finished speaking when he lunged suddenly at Steed, forcing him to move gingerly, cautiously, as he parried with his umbrella.

"Turkish rules?" Steed asked.

They fought, carefully fending each other off with civil little clashes of their weapons, back and forth, like fencing partners.

"If you insist," Sir August said. "And never forget that age and treachery will always overcome youth and skill."

"Then do try this." Steed dealt the madman a flurry of expert strokes, giving him a run for his money. Sir August had to work to hold his own, Steed saw with pleasure. His strength was his skillful lunge, but Steed and his umbrella had fought off many such attacks. It was, he reflected, old hat to him.

Tauntingly, Sir August said, "A man with an umbrella prays for rain."

Sir August laughed maniacally as Steed's brolly and his staff locked in a deadly face-off. Steed looked straight into the eyes of the man. From six inches away, it was quite a sight. Brilliance, madness, desire, and passion burned with enough intensity to make Steed blink.

"And a man without one is a fool. Never trust the weather, Sir August."

Sir August cocked his head, as if to correct Steed. "Rain or shine . . ."

With a masterful blow of his silver staff, Sir August struck Steed's umbrella away, sending it flying into the air above the maze.

". . . It's all mine."

Steed rolled his eyes. "Is that the best you can do? Such jingoism." Actually, he was a bit worried, and tried to gauge where and when the umbrella would fall.

Without it, he would be no more than a hospitable pincushion for Sir August's staff.

As he glanced up at the flying umbrella, he was aware
of movement, and looked down to see that Sir August
had vanished into the maze. Steed caught his brolly, ran
after Sir August, and promptly lost him.

"Mazes are not my forte," he murmured. "I shall
have to ask Dr. Darling to construct a practice course."
Steed turned the next corner, saw Emma running
toward him, and slowed, relieved. "There you are, Mrs.
Peel. You lead a merry—" But wait, he thought; something about the eyes . . .

Bad Emma, he realized, too late. She was already
in midair, executing a forward flip with a triple somersault flourish, her hands whirring and blurring like fan
blades . . . definitely superhuman, Steed thought, rather
like her twin in that respect. Then the blades struck him
in the face and he fell to the ground, unconscious.

Emma felt woozy, as if it were the morning after the
hunt ball. And she hadn't even opened her eyes yet.

When she did open them, slowly, experimentally,
she promptly closed them again. For the pattern of
wavy black-and-white lines, spinning fast enough to
make a fuzzy optical illusion of vibrating zigzags, was
enough to make anyone feel ill. Still half in a dream—or
nightmare—Emma blinked her eyes open again and
found that she was lying on a white brocade couch—
inside a glass cube. Mentally groaning, she wondered if
she were to be subjected to a nasty storm. Glass spheres,
glass cubes . . . there was no limit to Sir August's cre-
ativity where weather was concerned.

When she expanded her analysis to the rest of the
room, she found that she, the psychedelic pattern above
her, the lovely white couch, and the glass cube were
situated in the middle of a mirrored Louis XIV–style

ballroom. Mirrors covered every inch of the walls, reflecting the room and themselves endlessly in a dizzying succession. She couldn't quite tell where the room ended and where it began. Blinking again, not feeling quite herself, she heard a familiar voice.

"So glad you could come," Sir August said tenderly, from somewhere behind her head. She tried to sit up to face him, but found herself restrained by metal clamps over her forehead and neck, and straps lashing her wrists and ankles to the frame of the couch.

Coolly, she forced herself to smile. "Charmed, I'm sure."

Good thing she'd studied drama at university. Because, though she'd never let on, being confined in tight spaces was the one little problem she faced occasionally. That, and heights. This was . . . she was . . . she told herself to remain calm, that she'd been through much, much worse, and tried to breathe normally.

Sir August emerged from behind her head, dressed in a flowing white silk shirt that draped in a flattering way, revealing his enviable musculature. Emma had to admit, if it weren't for his madness, he might be rather attractive. His eyes twinkled with the suggestion of romance and desire. She looked at him and thought she had found the human embodiment of the being she'd always thought of as the devil himself: diabolically attractive, sinfully alluring, highly intelligent, immensely powerful, and unmistakably, utterly evil.

When his voice came, it was gentle. "Comfortable?" he asked.

"How cozy," Emma countered, trying to work out how to play this one. "Just the two of us."

"Like spoons in a drawer." His grin was lascivious.

"Perhaps I could help you," Emma offered. "If I knew what you wanted . . ."

Reason? Would that work?

"All in good time. I only want one thing. . . ."
She heard him take a long, shuddering breath. "You,
Emma."

All of her alarm bells went off simultaneously, but she
told herself she could use this. Yes, of course, this would
be easy. He was a man, thinking with the wrong part of
his anatomy—just like the rest of them. With testos-
terone for gray matter, they were lost.

"How touching," she said.

"Join me, Emma. And have the world."

She played for time. "You'd have to say 'please.' "

"But, of course," he smiled. "If you insist . . ."

Coyly, he moved closer. Puzzled, she saw him take
out his wallet. What now, she wondered? He selected a
tiny dart, less than two inches long, holding it by a silver
cupid at the end.

Oops . . . evidently she'd said something wrong. Poison, she wondered? Aphrodisiac? The cupid definitely
suggested . . .

Her eyes widened briefly at the horrors an aphrodisiac might bring, but then he aimed and plunged the
dart directly into her *heart*. He actually looked into her
eyes as he did it. She felt her body jolt as it hit, then immediately, an irresistible drowsiness. Sir August cocked
his head, watching her with great interest. Solicitude,
even. She fought to keep her eyes open, but they kept
falling . . . shut . . .

Good Lord, no, Emma thought . . . *not an aphrodisiac.* She would fight . . . she . . .

"Please?" His voice reached her ears in slow motion.
She kept forcing her eyes open when they closed . . . she
couldn't give in . . . he was watching her so closely . . .

"Uuuuuuhhhhhhh," she said involuntarily, her body
telling her to relax, to focus on Sir August. He . . . he . . .

She couldn't resist any longer, felt herself begin to
fade away. When her voice came, it was little more than

a whisper. "Your manners . . . leave . . . much . . . to be desired."

As she drifted away, she felt Sir August touch her cheek tenderly, bending over her, his breath hot.

No . . .

CHAPTER FIFTEEN

*My master through his art foresees the danger that
you, his friend, are in, and sends me forth (for else
his project dies) to keep them living.*

The Tempest, *William Shakespeare*

S teed opened his eyes; closed them again. His head . . .
Someone was shaking him urgently. . . .
He opened his eyes again, with effort, and saw Alice kneeling over him in the maze.

"I thought I was seeing double again."

"You were," Alice said. "A Gemini, definitely . . ."

Great Scott, Steed thought. *Not that rubbish again.*

"No time to lose," she continued. "Here's the plan. . . ."

Sir August peered down at Emma, hopelessly in love
with her. All the years he'd watched her on the Prospero
Program—the program *he'd* begun—using her brilliant
mind to its full advantage . . . and so beautiful, too.

There, she was drifting off. Feeling an intimacy with

her he'd only dreamed of, he whispered gently, close to her ear, "And when you awake, you will remember nothing . . . remember nothing . . . I, on the other hand, will remember only ecstasy. . . ."

It had hurt him to see her try to resist, squirming against her bonds. Quickly, he removed the straps and unclamped her head and neck. If she only knew the pleasure he would give her . . . Then, relieved, he saw her body relax completely, her eyes glaze over. She was his.

"Cloud . . ." he began, gently.

". . . shroud," she whispered.

It was working. Oh, the *years* he'd waited to try this particular aphrodisiac blend on her. Wide-eyed, he said, "Rain . . ."

It disturbed him to see her brow furrow, her lovely mouth turn down at the corners. ". . . pain."

"Moon . . ."

". . . June." Her voice was dreamy, barely there.

"August . . . ?" he tried.

Her mouth opened, she tried, but no word would come. Sir August leaned urgently over her, his need growing. . . .

In a singsong voice, Emma said, "August is a lovely month, lovely as can be. First it loved poor Peter, now it's loving me. . . ." The rhyme faded into silence as Emma stared into space, her mouth tantalizingly open. Those lips, he thought . . . so perfect . . .

"Perfect. *Perfect*," he said, breathing fast. He moved closer, lowering his lips to hers. So close now, so close . . . after all these years . . . He closed his eyes, contemplating, relishing the moment. Brushing her lips with his, he inhaled deeply, treasuring the scent of her perfume, then pursed his lips in a tender, lingering kiss.

Sir August moved back, enjoying the suspense. Only moments now until his dream would be fulfilled. Misty-eyed, he lifted her finger to his lips, brushing it across them, tasting her. He sighed deeply, then stood.

"Monsoon time," he said, and lifted the needle of a nearby gramophone, already spinning, onto the vinyl. The first tender phrases of Sibelius's "Valse Triste" drifted into the room. As if by magic, Emma rose from the couch, stepped down from the glass cube, and advanced toward Sir August.

He clasped her to him. Ah, this was heaven! With his hand on her slender waist, smelling the supple leather of her suit, he was enraptured. He spun her in a slow waltz, her hair flying, its scent in his nostrils. This was the best prelude he'd ever found to . . .

Sir August gazed deeply into Emma's eyes, sweeping her round and round the room, gradually floating toward the huge, ornate high-backed divan in the corner. Gently, he waltzed her over, and laid her down on the burgundy velvet. She didn't resist as he buried his head in her breast, smelling the leather and the perfume, and—yes! That essential bit of sweat.

"Ahhhrrrrrmmmm," he breathed, smashing his face into her skin, his tongue licking the smooth slope where the curve of her breasts began. He couldn't bear it any longer. Pulling his face off of her chest, he reached with shaking fingers for the ring at the top of the zipper to her catsuit. By all that was barometric, he'd never felt such desire. . . .

Relishing the sound of the zipper unzipping as he slowly pulled the metal ring down, past her breasts, past her ribs, encased in the smooth muscles he'd admired for so long—how he loved a really *strong* woman—then the precious little indentation of her waist—there was nothing on between her and the catsuit!—and finally toward her most enticing part, the part he wasn't sure he'd ever . . . At last, he hovered over her, staring at the expanse of her creamy, ivory skin against the naughty black leather . . .

The front doorbell rang.

Disbelieving, Sir August willed it to stop. It wasn't that he had any intention of answering it. Nothing meant anything to him compared to Emma Peel. But it was distracting, and these matters of love were delicate. . . . The deafening sound reverberated through the house, echoing long after it had been released. He wouldn't let it ruin this moment.

But some maniac was ringing it again, holding it down. At this of all times!

He ignored the noise as best he could, but then the needle stuck on the Sibelius record, repeating the same five notes over and over. The mood was gone.

"Someone's going to pay for this!" he muttered, teeth clenched. Swearing furiously, he headed for the door of the mirrored room. In his fury, he slammed the massive, carved wooden door behind him before striding into the hall. Where were his useless household staff? Why didn't they answer the . . . bloody hell. He'd let them all go, in anticipation of his tryst with Emma.

Brrrriiiinnnngggg! The bell-ringer was incessant, persistent, just asking to be dispatched, Sir August thought. He charged down the hall like the angry bear he was, his swearing increasing in volume, each step thudding furiously on the parquet floor. Whoever had done this . . .

The bell rang yet again as he reached for the door handle. He swung it open with murderous intent—only to see a kindly, gray-haired little old lady wearing an apologetic smile.

Enraged, he watched as she said, "Raffle tickets, church fete. Do come."

Summoning all his self-control, he managed to mutter, "Not today, thanks." He couldn't very well throttle a little old lady from the parish church.

He began to close the door, but she peeked round the edge. "Tombola, Lucky Dip, Pin the Tail on the Donkey . . ." she sang enticingly.

"Or *any* day," he finished, seething. He swung the door shut decisively, but she stuck her oxblood brogue between it and the door frame.

Incredulous, exasperated, Sir August opened it slightly again as she spoke. "Poor Reverend Arbuthnot. His organ needs help. Perhaps a small donation . . . ?"

Sir August frowned menacingly, wishing he could garrote the old hag.

"If you're going to be difficult," she said, narrowing her eyes, "I'll have to insist." He saw her reach into her sensible leather handbag, double-strapped like the Queen Mother's, and produce a magnum handgun. Staring down into the small black eye of the gun barrel, he heard her say, "Where's Mrs. Peel?"

CHAPTER SIXTEEN

Awake, dear heart, awake, thou hast slept well; awake.

Prospero, in The Tempest, *William Shakespeare*

The slam of the door roused Emma with a start. Where . . . ? The first thing she saw was her own naked body, the creamy expanse of her skin lying as if on display upon the velvet-covered sofa. With an effort, she reached for the zipper—unzipped to its fullest extent, she noticed with a sick feeling—and pulled the ring right the way up to her neck. With revulsion, she thought of Sir August and the aphrodisiac dart. She didn't remember anything after that. Where was he?

She sat up; the room spun. Putting her hands to her head to try to still the whirlies, she tried to stand, but staggered, her balance off. She glued her eyes to the door at the side of the room and wove toward it, nearly overbalancing several times along the way. Finally she put her hands out and leaned against the wall. Whatever was on the tip of that dart had been potent stuff, Emma decided.

She wasn't sure how far she could make it, tipsy as she was, but knew she had to try. She pulled the door open, falling over onto her backside as she overcompensated. She got woozily to her feet, crashing against the doorjamb on her way out of the mirrored chamber. Everything floated round her as she reeled down the corridor, heading away from Sir August's booming voice at the front door. Bouncing off the walls, which seemed to move in and out as she breathed, she threw herself toward the next door she saw to the outside, but found herself in yet another room.

Confused, she went back out of the room, bruising her hip on the door frame as she smacked into it, and closed the door. Where was the door to the outside . . . ? Definitely funny stuff, that potion. She opened another door down the corridor, in the direction of the one that she'd thought led outside, but it was the room she had just left. The exterior door had somehow ceased to exist.

Emma frowned, left the room, closing the door, and tried the next door down the hallway. Again, uncannily, the exact same room. "I'm going out of my mind," she breathed, and retreated to the corridor, leaving the door open this time as she ran, struggling to keep her balance, nearly panic-stricken. She was stuck . . . inside . . .

Way down the corridor, she tried another door. Same room. She looked at the nightmarish room spinning around her and felt burning behind her eyes.

Bad Emma giggled as she watched Mrs. Peel on the video screen of the security room. This was fun. The woman was staggering about like a drunkard, unable to find her way out of the maze of rooms Bad Emma had activated. It had taken Bad Emma a while to become familiar with the technology, but once she'd grasped the idea of Sir August's virtual rooms, she'd found herself quite competent at manipulating them. And she'd spent so many days following him about, watching him. That had been her real training.

It was all a matter of projecting computer-generated images of rooms from hidden projectors and of spinning entire sections of the house about on rotating platforms. If she wanted to, she could keep the woman running desperately for days, always moving the exit further and further out of reach.

Bad Emma's eyes gleamed as she saw despair on the other Emma's face. She brought the camera's focus in tight on the woman's visage, and delighted in the horror she saw there. Perhaps Mrs. Peel suffered from a bit of claustrophobia . . . ah! That gave her a wonderful idea.

Manipulating the joystick controls of the room dimension system, she began to move the walls closer together. She did it slowly, gleefully, delighting in the fact that Mrs. Peel would wonder if she were merely *imagining* the ever-so-subtle narrowing of the room, considering her altered state. Bad Emma next narrowed the room in the other direction. She thought Mrs. Peel would notice now. Focusing in on her eyes again, Bad Emma laughed uproariously. The woman looked positively terrified as she stared incredulously at the walls—almost as if her eyes would pop out of her skull.

Right. Now for some *real* fun. Bad Emma brought the walls in, then out. In even farther, then out again. She repeated the process a dozen or more times, until finally she made the room a mere five feet on all sides— even the ceiling height was five feet. Bad Emma knew from her own identical height that Mrs. Peel was five feet nine inches tall. She had to crouch, like an animal, Bad Emma noticed with satisfaction.

As she considered her next torture, Bad Emma thought with disgust that she had to give the woman credit, much as she despised her. There had been no sobbing, no screaming, no carrying-on as so many other humans would have done in the same situation. For the first time she began to understand why Sir August cared for Mrs. Peel so obsessively.

And that made her all the more determined to dispose of her.

Heights, Bad Emma thought. She'd seen the terror on the woman's face when she'd been pinned to the edge of the rooftop. She thought for a moment, her eyes on the woman in the monitor. Yes. She'd toy with her a bit more, make the room large again. If she used that room with the huge mirror on one wall, Emma might go over to look at it, and she'd make it appear to be the edge of a cliff. When she looked through it, she'd see a precipitous drop-off—perhaps like that from the top of the Matterhorn.

The only possible drawback, Bad Emma reflected, was that the real glass mirror, onto which she would only project the frightening view when Mrs. Peel got really close, was on an actual exterior wall. And there was a real window behind it. But there was no chance that the woman would suss that out. She'd be in such a state by then . . .

Bad Emma made the walls of the room larger, saw Mrs. Peel stand tall again. Bad Emma saw that she was visibly relieved. "Not for long, dear," she said with a smile. She spun the mirror room into place and removed the projected walls. Now Mrs. Peel was really in a room, the one with the mirror in it.

Bad Emma sat back in her chair to watch. Her finger

was poised atop the button that would project a view from a narrow Alpine pass. She could hardly wait.

To her satisfaction, Mrs. Peel started toward the mirror immediately.

Steed had to get into the house; had to get to Mrs. Peel. God only knew what disaster had befallen her. The thought of her facing whatever it was bravely, fearlessly, was enough to make him desperate. But he seemed to be trapped in a maze of buildings now, instead of shrubbery. He darted round the corner of one wing of Hallucinogen Hall, only to find himself back where he started. Stopping, he gazed at a window. Something decidedly odd about it. Tapping it with his finger, he found it was hard stone, merely *painted* to look like a window. He knew that paint effects were all the rage at the moment, but really, this seemed going a bit far. The thing looked incredibly real.

Steed shook his head and started to move toward what he *thought* was the back of the house. He went round the west wing, turned past the garden and . . . found himself right back where he'd started. He moved again toward the wall of trompe l'oeil glass and started tapping. . . .

Bailey entered the sitting room, about to demand what all the fuss was about, when he saw Alice holding Sir August at bay with an impressive gun. Sir August didn't give him away as he sneaked up behind her, raising the cosh he kept on his belt.

He connected nicely with her skull, and the old woman fell with a *thunk* onto the hardwood floor, her gun tumbling and sliding across the polished surface.

Granny never knew what hit her, Bailey thought,

laughing. He looked at Sir August, expecting praise, and his smile faded. The master looked as if he would gladly kill him, his eyes shooting daggers as he leaped from the room.

"Some thanks I get," Bailey muttered, huffing as he picked up Granny's lovely black automatic.

Emma heard a cacophony of bizarre noises and put her hands over her ears. If everything would only stop spinning . . . someone was tapping somewhere; somewhere else, laughing, a sinister laugh; shuffling feet; a tinkling music box; Sir August's voice, repeating over and over . . .

She was going mad.

Emma made for the stairs in the center of the room that had been driving her barmy. She climbed, hoping it would take her out of the room, out of this bizarre trap. The staircase spun beneath her feet. She tripped, grasped the handrail, and hung there for a moment, out of breath. Still in that room!

She started to climb again, not a moment to lose, but the stairs kept coming and coming, as if they were multiplying above her. The spinning and the running were all too much, and in desperation, she looked up, for a way out.

She stopped, reeling, and clung to a baluster as she stared at the ceiling. It had been painted in the classical style, clearly inspired by *The Tempest*. Four cherubic zephyrs blew winds from their own directions, with a four-pointed compass at the center.

The tapping grew louder; Emma hesitated. Looking round her again, she saw that she was now standing on the floor of the room . . . no stairs at all . . . but the room was growing smaller.

Was she imagining it, because of her fear of closed-in spaces? Or was it the aphrodisiac cocktail Sir August had administered? But she could swear that . . . yes, now she could see that the walls were, in fact, literally closing in on her. How was it possible?

She blinked as the room expanded, contracted, then expanded once again. She'd be certifiable if this continued. It was some sort of trap, she told herself, some plaything of Sir August's. She merely had to remain calm, and she'd find her way out of this as well.

But then the apparently endless expansion and contraction of the room came to an end, and to Emma's horror, it came to rest at a mere five feet in width and length. Then, anticipating the worst, she looked up as the ceiling descended. It touched the top of her head, pressing inexorably down, and still down. Emma crouched as it came lower, refusing to kneel. That would be a posture of weakness, of supplication. She fought for calm, finding a bit of strength to cling to in her anger. It made her angry that someone, somehow, had divined her greatest weakness and was preying upon it. She wouldn't give them the satisfaction. It was Sir August, no doubt.

Just then it stopped. So perhaps the room wouldn't crush her, after all. She waited for several minutes as nothing further happened, wondering what the game was. She watched, fascinated, as the room suddenly returned to its original size, yet seemed to change. The ceiling moldings were different, for one thing, and the painting on the ceiling was back. She did a double take as a huge mirror appeared on the far wall—the one she would have judged to be the exterior wall, if she could still have trusted her sense of direction, and the painted cherubs above her.

She started toward it, struggling to remain calm. If the room started to collapse on her again, she didn't know . . . Scanning in all four directions, she decided she had no choice but to take a gamble. Blindly, staggering, she ran in the direction the compass said was south. She ran, weaving, tripping, toward the tall wall mirror. She saw herself in the mirror, running toward herself. Summoning all her remaining strength, she threw herself at the mirror in a somersaulting leap, not knowing if she would be successful because of the dizziness.

In the moment before she struck the glass, as she was flying toward it, she saw a breathtaking panorama of mountains with a deep, deep valley below. She felt panic overwhelm her, the fear of catapulting into space filling her with despair. It was too late—she was flying. . . .

She heard the crash of the glass as she hit it sideways, her somersault sliding off balance, felt little bits of the mirror stinging her face and hands. She expected to fall endlessly through space, but after a mere two seconds she had landed on her back, hard, outside, the wind knocked out of her. The mirror had been a *window* . . . ?

Suddenly Steed in his bowler loomed over her.

"Steed!" Groggily, she got to her hands and knees, struggled to her feet. She couldn't let him see that she . . . oh . . .

Stumbling toward him, trying to focus on the diagonal stripes of his old school tie, her body failed her. She felt his strong arms catch her as she pitched toward the ground, smelled a whiff of his cologne.

Steed . . .

Sir August tried to soothe his thwarted passion in the mirrored chamber in which he had left Emma. When he'd returned, half an hour ago now, she was gone. Why did the woman have to be so damnably intelligent? Winding up a ticking clock, he held it to his ear, and recited to himself, "My charms crack not, my spirits obey, and time/ Goes upright with his carriage . . . How's the day?"

Behind him, on the divan, was Bad Emma. His creation. He regarded her through one of the room's many mirrors, and shook his head. Sometimes he feared he'd made her just a wee bit too intelligent. She'd been getting out of line lately. Look at her, he thought, trying to be like Emma. Pitiful. Disgusting.

She lounged on the divan, some horrendous red laquer on her fingernails, clad in a lacy black bodystocking. Her figure was perfect, technically—a precise duplicate of Emma's. Her only flaw was that she wasn't Emma Peel.

Standing, she faced him, posing like a Victoria's Secret model, woodenly trying to mouth the words she'd heard Emma say: "Cumulus . . . Stratocumulus . . . Nimbus . . ." She mangled the pronunciation of the words, while smiling enticingly at him.

Sir August turned on her, furious. He stalked over to her until his face was nearly touching hers and spoke quietly. "I don't want *you*. I could make hundreds of you. Thousands." Suddenly, his voice exploded at top volume. *"Bring her back!"*

Sulking, he stormed out of the room, stopping only to hurl his clock at the mirror, which shattered violently, crumbling into a million pieces, leaving Bad Emma's reflection in shards.

That was it, Bad Emma thought. She was going to get rid of Emma Peel once and for all. Then she, Bad Emma, would be all he had left. He would have no choice but to love her.

Ripping off the black lace bodystocking she'd ordered specially from Paris, she threw it, shredded, on the floor next to her. He should have given her better learning software; her neural nets simply weren't up to acquiring meteorological terms at the drop of a hat. She wondered why he had neglected this area when he'd taken such pains to program subjective human feelings into her, such as competition and loyalty. An artificial intelligence genius like Sir August should have known not to skimp on the brain.

She sighed. She would have to work hard to be an authentic Emma Peel, after she'd killed the woman. Perhaps if she studied very hard, she could convince him that she *was* Emma Peel. There were plenty of books in the library . . . yes, she was certain she could do it if she applied herself.

The main problem was getting rid of the woman. Bad Emma's strength was far superior, he'd seen to that. She felt pride at the thought. But the damnable woman didn't give up without a fight. Bad Emma couldn't believe that she'd actually found a way out through the window. Who would have guessed that she'd charge straight through her worst fears? Into the arms of the man who kept rescuing her? At least temporarily, the real Emma Peel did possess far greater intelligence than Bad Emma.

Damn her! She still had to acquire more swear words. Her limited vocabulary of them gave her such satisfaction. Damn, damn, damn. Emma stalked, naked, to her quarters upstairs and at the rear of the Hall, her fury building. Once in the tiny room that used to belong to a kitchen maid, with its peeling wallpaper and faded furniture, she pulled on her black leather catsuit again— what the real Emma was wearing that day. Then she practiced in the mirror, contorting her mouth to imitate Emma's. It was the real Emma's smile that got him, she knew. It was the same smile he'd had the painter capture in the portrait in the organ room—a little twist at the corner of the lips. She thought the English word for that expression was "wry," though her lexicon suggested "bitter" and "ironic" as well.

Bad Emma tried then to twist her lips at the edge,

but ended up looking like a moping child. She tried again and again, until even she realized it looked like a rather nasty facial tic. With a cry of rage, she gave up on the "wry" smile and moved on to the expression in the eyes.

Moving closer to the mirror, she tried for the warmth and—well, flash—that Emma had in her eye. "Sparkle," her lexicon said. She didn't know how to *make* sparkle, and kept watching her eyes as she widened and narrowed them, opened and closed them, but they wouldn't sparkle. They looked metallic, which was appropriate, because they were made largely of stainless steel. Emma bashed her hand into the mirror, then realized that had been stupid. Now she would have to practice in the broken bits.

Her neural net made a new association. Perhaps there were contact lenses . . . the same kind Sir August had embedded in her eyes to make them the same icy blue as Emma's. Yes. She would search for "sparkle" contact lenses.

She took one last long look in the mirror. With her new facial tic and dead-looking eyes, she had to admit she was no match for the real Emma. There was no option but to kill the woman, though she'd been instructed not to do so without orders. At that thought, a more authentic smile spread across her lips. Now *this* smile wasn't bad, she thought. Not bad at all. The idea dawned as her neural nets made the linkages that allowed her to learn: a smile came from *within*, from what a person was thinking . . . it was a difficult concept to grasp. All such subjective human things were. She'd explore that more later.

Oh, yes, she thought as she strapped on her boots. She'd find a way to dispose of her. If not today, soon. As she inserted and affixed her weapons to various spots on her anatomy, she thought one of her masters might even order her to kill the woman. In that case, Sir August couldn't be angry when he found out Bad Emma had killed her. And then he would be all hers.

With a genuine smile, she checked the poison gas canister in her cleavage and tripped lightly down the narrow servants' stairway.

CHAPTER SEVENTEEN

. . . make yourself ready in your cabin for the
mischance of the hour, if it so hap.
Cheerly, good hearts!

The Tempest, *William Shakespeare*

Steed thought he saw Emma's eyelids flutter, and hurried over to the daybed. Yes, she was coming round. He'd begun to worry; it had been hours and hours . . . not that he hadn't enjoyed having her there.

She put a hand to her head and twisted suddenly in alarm, unsure of her surroundings.

"Don't worry," he said, sitting gently next to her. "You're at my flat. Quite safe . . ."

She looked round the flat. Steed wondered what she thought of it. It was mostly leather and mahogany, with well-stocked library shelves to the ceiling, oil portraits of his ancestors, and Regency furniture. He'd never really considered it before; it was tradition, the way of the Steeds. It was all he knew. Momentarily disquieted by the thought that he might possibly have chosen something else, he saw his furnishings with new eyes.

She frowned, confused. "What am I doing here?"

"Having tea."

"Is that all?"

"After a manner of speaking."

Emma looked at him skeptically.

"Your boots . . . a delivery from Trubshaw's. They may come in useful. Allow me."

He presented her with a pair of black leather knee-boots, containing, unbeknownst to her, a hidden micro-tag. He hoped she wouldn't mind the slight decep-tion, but he needed to be able to find her when he needed her.

Emma ran her hands over the fine kid leather, look-ing a bit more herself, Steed thought.

"I was worried. What happened to you?" Steed knelt to help her on with the boots, brushing the leather appreciatively.

She thought for a moment. "I remember the maze, a house, music, Sir August, then . . . nothing."

"Try to remember," Steed urged. "It's very impor-tant. Alice was on to something, and the Ministry will want to find out. You're in extreme danger. You'd better stay here with me."

Emma raised her eyebrows at him. "Is that wise?"

He chose to ignore her implication. She did play hard to get. "You'll be safer here," he went on. "We can talk it over. An official debriefing. With no interruptions."

She smiled. "You live alone?"

He nodded.

"No Mrs. Steed?" she asked.

He slid his hand over Emma's boot, caressing her leg, taking his time about answering. He moved closer to her, smelling her subtle scent. Perhaps a trace of Ysatis by Givenchy, he thought. His face very close to hers, he said, "Mrs. Steed lives in Wiltshire." He felt her stiffen. "My mother."

She relaxed, and he felt her move closer still. "I had you down as a creature of habit. A bachelor's life."

"It's worked quite well, until now." He touched a finger next to her mouth, ran it down her creamy skin.

"Don't tell me. You never met the right girl." She quivered; he felt it run through her like an electrical current.

"There's always the exception. . . ." He played with her hair, loosely twisting a handful of her shiny auburn tresses. She was the most beautiful, intelligent, capable, supremely *English* woman he had ever met.

". . . That proves the rule?" Their faces were so close, he could feel the heat from her.

"Quite," he said. "You're exceptional in many things. But duty first. Shall we make a start?"

With delight, he saw that she took his meaning, leaning into him. "A time and place for everything," she murmured, her lips touching his.

"Now is definitely the time," he said, closing his eyes.

"And the place?" Emma finished.

Slowly, Steed, still kneeling, drew closer yet, leaning toward her as she sat. Their bodies touched; his one hand still caressed her foot through her boot. He could feel her toes through the leather. He felt his face flush, betraying him.

"Too tight," Emma said.

"Push," he breathed, ready to kiss her.

There was a knock at the door.

Crestfallen, they opened their eyes and drew apart as the door flew open. Before Steed could move, a familiar voice said, "Hello, Steed."

Father. Steed swiveled round to see her with Dr. Darling and two Ministry agents, who went immediately to Emma. Damn it all; this was the limit. No courtesy. No respect for others' privacy. What was the world coming to?

"I believe it's normal for guests to knock," he said, in high dudgeon.

The agents hustled Emma out as Steed looked on, distressed.

"We can dispense with formalities, Steed. I want Mrs. Peel." Father's black glasses intensified her sinister demeanor, Steed thought. "Interrogation."

Behind Father, Brenda pushed Mother into view, looking desolate. "Nothing I can do about it, Steed. Out of my hands."

"Security restriction, Steed. You, too. Mrs. Peel is under arrest."

God only knew what they'd do to her, Steed thought. He'd never minded when it was the enemy, but Mrs. Peel . . .

He followed them out the mews door, torturing himself. Why hadn't he realized that Father might do something like this? He was responsible. He should never have brought her to his flat. In the cobbled courtyard, Steed watched in anguish as the agents bundled Emma into a Ministry car. Not good, thought Steed. Not good at all. Mother, Dr. Darling, and Brenda looked on, with apologetic glances at Steed.

Emma glanced back at him as the car pulled away, and he held her eyes for a long moment. He hoped she read in his eyes that he would return for her. They both knew that people suspected of treason rarely came out of the Ministry's interrogation cells alive.

Nearly beside himself, Steed became aware of Brenda hovering behind him. "Sorry, John," she said sadly. "Father's in control. Always wanted Mother off the case."

"Only one place to go," he said, grimly determined.

"I'll fix it," Brenda said, eager to please. "I can be very persuasive. You only have to ask, John. Whenever, wherever . . ."

"I'll keep that in mind." He supposed that someday

he would have to tell her that they had no future. But it was so nice to have a pleasant face in the office, and she didn't seem to take his hints. He certainly couldn't deal with it now, with Mrs. Peel in mortal danger.

He stared after the car that took Emma away from him.

CHAPTER EIGHTEEN

Misery acquaints a man with strange bedfellows.
The Tempest, *William Shakespeare*

Brenda had been as good as her word. She'd fixed the appointment, and Steed found himself striding down yet another subterranean corridor in the Ministry. It was a tunnel, really, its curved ceiling not unlike that of a tube station, merely lower. Water dripped from the ceiling in great, heavy drops. He dodged them as best he could . . . bad for the suit.

Why was so much of their work underground, anyway? Sighing, he had to admit it was logical. Their secrets were never to see the light of day, likewise, the agents. Perhaps it was all intended to send a subliminal message.

At last he came to a door, so dark and unremarkable he was amazed anyone knew it was there. In small black letters someone had painted on the door: Room 282,

Colonel I. Jones, Archives. Steed knocked. No one answered.

"Helloooo?" he called.

No answer. Steed gripped the door handle and poked his nose inside.

From nowhere in particular that Steed could see, a voice called, "Hello?"

Steed cast about for the speaker, but couldn't see anyone. "Hello?" he tried again.

"Talk to the pipe. That usually helps." Across the room, a pipe puffed in midair, unattached to any human encumbrance. Suddenly a match flamed to life, and moved down into the pipe bowl.

Unusual, thought Steed.

The match flew into an ashtray, apparently on its own.

Most unusual. Still, there were many eccentric people in the Ministry . . . all of them, really. "Colonel Jones?" Steed inquired.

"Don't worry about me being invisible," came a voice from across the room, moving toward him. "Other than that I'm perfectly normal."

"I see."

"Or rather, you don't." He chuckled. "Learnt the trick in camouflage. Till the accident made a prang of things. Tucked away in the bloody basement now. Lucky if we even get the tea trolley. . . ."

Delicately, Steed cut in. "Sorry, but I don't have much time. I want you to take a look at this map, please." He pulled out the BROLLY map and held it out in the direction of the pipe. "And I need to know more about the Prospero Program and something called Gemini."

Steed had been wearing mental sackcloth and ashes ever since he'd realized that Alice had tried to tell him about Gemini. To think that he'd assumed the elderly woman was raving a bit, never guessing that she held the key to their whole disastrous problem. How he hated to admit that he'd underestimated her. Now both she and Emma were paying the price.

Steed sat miserably on a chair opposite a disorderly metal desk that had once been painted a dismal green. Behind the desk, where the pipe drifted, a chair suddenly swiveled and a drawer rolled open. A file popped up and floated through the air.

"So you want to know about the Gemini Project. I have a digestive here somewhere. . . ." Colonel Jones handed Steed a biscuit of the promised variety, along with a cup of tea. A spoonful of sugar followed it through the air.

"Most kind," Steed mumbled. How could he sit and swill Earl Grey while Emma languished in a Ministry cell? He tried to keep the impatience out of his voice. "You see, this really is rather urgent, Colonel Jones."

"Call me 'Colonel'—no standing on ceremony." He lifted the BROLLY map into the air. "Hmm. Let's take a look." The chair shifted back, the map rose, and Steed followed invisible steps that tapped away from him. As the colonel turned a corner, Steed followed him through the door, down yet another dim tunnel. Their two sets of footsteps echoed grimly, bouncing off the walls.

"The Gemini Project," the colonel said suddenly. "Ah, yes."

Steed followed him into a corridor off the tunnel, which was stuffed with filing cabinets brimming over with foolscap files. Steed found it remarkable that anything could ever be found here, with files and papers layered like geological strata. The colonel led him through double doors into the library. It was foggy in the room, or was it dust?

"Achooo!" Steed's nasal membranes informed him that the air was, indeed, filled with dust. Steed looked round in amazement. Tall wooden shelves stretched up to the ceiling, and boxes stamped "Top Secret" spilled over with loose papers.

The colonel took out his torch and proceeded to search through it all, starting haphazardly in the center of the middle shelf. "A place for everything, and everything in its place," he said inexplicably. "Happy hunting."

Steed, undaunted, glanced at his watch and began to dig through the first box on the first shelf.

Hang on, Emma, he thought. *I'm coming.*

Father stepped onto the glass gallery and spoke through the intercom. She had never enjoyed going to the Ministry's psychiatric hospital until that day, but she was definitely enjoying herself now. "Hello, Mrs. Peel," her icy voice rang out. "Welcome back to the Ministry."

She could picture Emma below in the padded cell. She'd heard the physical description, and wasn't surprised Auggie found her so attractive. For years and years she'd played second fiddle to this Emma Peel, though Auggie had needed *her*, Father, as his partner. Well, he wouldn't have Emma Peel to lust after any more, she thought. Perhaps he'd see Father through new eyes. . . .

Father stared in the direction of Emma's cell. She'd been told that the padded vinyl inside these ultrahigh security cubicles was bright, neon orange, designed to weaken the prisoner by its very garishness. She wondered if the oh-so-clever Mrs. Peel had figured out she was in a top-secret interrogation cell. She hoped it would get good and nasty.

"Dr. Darling confirmed his diagnosis," she said into the intercom. "You're suffering from delusions. An extreme psychotic personality disorder. A classic syndrome to overcome your subconscious guilt . . . Would you like to sit down?"

"Thank you, I'm fine hanging around." The woman

sounded disturbingly composed, Father thought. She'd specially issued the order for the woman to be placed in this, the smallest cell, because their surveillance of her deep background had indicated there might be a tendency toward claustrophobia. Well, she'd see what she could do to knock Mrs. Peel off her even keel.

"We need to talk," Father began.

"About the weather? How topical. Or should I say tropical?"

Fresh little tart, this Mrs. Peel. "It'll help pass the time," Father said, her irritation growing.

Then, something happened that puzzled Father. Emma Peel began to speak, rapidly, as if forcing herself to recover her reason, to demonstrate that she was all right.

"Time would pass anyway, if you think about it logically. But then, so few do think logically, or even antilogically. Clockwise or anticlockwise, tick-tock tock-tick, seesaw Margery Daw, it amounts to the same thing. After all, how do you know I'm the real Mrs. Peel?"

Father smiled. Oh, yes; they were quite sure they had the right Mrs. Peel. But . . . perhaps the cell had worked rather better than she thought, insanitywise. Or was she bluffing?

"How real do you *feel*, Mrs. Peel?" Father asked, grinning. Perhaps she could push her over the top.

Mrs. Peel seemed to accelerate her insane logic. "I'll repeat the question, bypassing the weather—which, no doubt, being British, we'll return to in a moment. Do I walk like Mrs. Peel, talk like Mrs. Peel? Am I witty, wise, wonderful to know? Or do I go round shooting Ministry agents and attempting to rule the world on my days off? No doubt about it, logically or even antilogically, by definition, whatever the weather, I'm going mad."

Father frowned. "Now you're playing games." She thought she felt a cold, and quite sane, stare from Mrs.

Peel. Well. Time to have a bit of fun herself. In the distance, Big Ben chimed the hour as Father pressed a button and exited the gallery, moving down the stairway toward the cells. Smiling, she motioned to Bad Emma, who'd been waiting in the hallway. The two of them walked to the end cell, Mrs. Peel's, where Father pressed another button. The door to the tiny cubicle slid open. The two stepped in, and the door slid shut after them.

Father could feel the tension in the air as the two Emmas regarded each other with utter hatred. She wished she could see it, but didn't really need to. The hostility was palpable. Father snapped her fingers at Bad Emma, who produced the canister of gas. Before another word was spoken, Bad Emma had pressed the pump in front of the prisoner with a satisfying *ppppffffffffftttt!*

Father heard the woman's body fall, unconscious, against the vinyl.

Well. That was that, then.

CHAPTER NINETEEN

What seest thou else in the dark backward and abysm of time?

The Tempest, *William Shakespeare*

Back in Colonel Invisible Jones's "front" office, the projector beam played on a miraculously uncluttered patch of wall, illuminating a slide of Sir August, smiling with "Dolly" and "Dolly"—two cloned sheep, according to the slide's label. It was one of many that Steed and the colonel had found pertaining to Gemini and Prospero. The filing system had actually worked, to Steed's amazement.

Sipping his third cup of tea, Steed used his left hand to flip through pages of a Gemini Twins report in the dim light of the colonel's desk lamp. The clones possessed human anatomy as well as supplemental biocircuitry, according to the report. Colonel Jones passed him another file as Steed reprimanded himself for being so dense.

"Gemini . . . Gemini . . . of *course*. A Ministry cloning experiment. Sir August ran it, but it appears he went too far. They pulled him off."

"But Sir August was under Ministry surveillance after Gemini," the colonel interjected.

A file whisked through the air toward Steed. He caught it as the colonel flicked the projector button, bringing up a slide of a young Sir August with an even younger Father. She'd actually been relatively attractive once, Steed noted with surprise. The colonel clicked up a slide of bulleted Gemini goals, then Prospero goals, complete with specifics such as location sites for transmitters. One of them included the Serpentine Lake.

"Surveillance—by Father?"

"Yes," the colonel replied. "Sir August could only set up Prospero after Father gave him an 'all clear.' So Mrs. Peel never knew."

"I see," Steed said. "So when Mother took over at the Ministry, Sir August joined forces with Father. . . ."

"Eeny-meeny-miny-mole. Bingo!" The colonel blew a smoke ring into the air and moved in front of the projector beam. Steed noted with interest that the invisible man did have a shadow. If only H. G. Wells were alive to see it . . .

"It's all in here, Colonel. Why didn't you ever tell anyone?"

"Nobody ever asked."

The invisible man blew smoke upward toward a glass grate in the ceiling. With surprise, Steed noticed it was covered in snow. He frowned. "Is it my imagination, or is it getting colder in here?"

Outside, it was dusk. The temperature had plunged to an unearthly fifteen degrees Fahrenheit, hardly the norm for July fifteenth. An eerie stillness prevailed, and the people of London had realized that something dangerously sinister was afoot. News reporters had recommended that everyone return home and remain indoors until further notice, so the normally vivacious city appeared to have been evacuated, as in wartime.

The once-teeming streets were deserted. Empty taxis lined Oxford Street; tour buses sat vacant in Trafalgar Square. Harrods had sent everyone home, having to push, literally, a dozen American diehards out the door. The door of All Souls on Regent Street had been padlocked, an unprecedented occurrence; even the meat market at Smithfield had packed up. Fish and chips shops were battened down all over Whitechapel, their sliding steel grates firmly in place.

It didn't bode well.

A wind kicked up, blowing paper down the streets. Leaves fluttered on the trees. Birds flew for shelter, and a weather vane began to spin ominously. At Hyde Park, the surface of the Serpentine was ruffled, and the boathouse bore a hastily scrawled sign that read, "Closed until further notice."

Black-bottomed clouds scudded past, casting dark shadows on the ground. Flocks of pigeons zigzagged through the sky, migrating to a gentler, kinder place—a place where people still threw breadcrumbs.

In Buckingham Palace, the Queen looked out from her private chamber, frowning. The weather certainly was unseasonably cool, especially for Saint Swithin's Day. Cloudy, too. And everyone knew what *that* meant . . . if the weather was bad today, that meant the next forty days would be rainy as well. Such unfortunate timing . . . they were due to leave for the family holiday at Balmoral in a few days. Scottish weather was difficult enough, without a bad Saint Swithin's Day. And her corgis felt their rheumatism so much more when it was cold. . . .

She shivered. This was the only drawback to her kingdom. The bally miserable weather. If not for that, her sceptred isle would be perfect. She sighed. If only all those lovely tropical islands hadn't proclaimed their independence, she could move the family holiday to one of them. Permanently. But tradition was strong. What would the nation do if they saw her cavorting on some white sand beach in a bathing costume instead of stalwartly trekking across the heathery fields in her tweeds, corgis hot on the heels of her sensible shoes? No, she'd have to stick with tradition.

Perhaps someday someone would be able to do something about the blasted weather. Surely with all the money they'd invested in that secret weather research program, something was bound to be forthcoming. Though now they'd managed to muck that up as well, blown up the whole expensive facility. She shook her head, wishing they'd pull their socks up and get on with it. Until then, they'd just have to put a brave face on it and muddle through somehow.

Behind the boathouse at the Serpentine, Bailey and his thugs placed the glittering silver transmitter on the ground, anchoring it there with spikes that folded out for the purpose. Bailey turned the transmitter's black dial, and it emitted two distinct beeps. A display flashed the neon green words: "Transmitter ON."

Bailey knew that the transmitter at his feet would communicate with another like it, hidden among the trees on Serpentine Island, opposite the boathouse. He heard a responding *beep-beep* from across the water and knew that everything was ready.

He plucked the radio off his belt. "Ariel to Prospero. Ariel to Prospero. The Serpentine is *Magic*. I repeat, the Serpentine is *Magic*."

• • •

Sir August leaned against the wainscoting of the paneled meeting room and licked the ice lolly he'd bought from a shop on the street. Somehow, a White Chocolate Avalanche had sounded the very thing. Shaking his head, he watched the feathers fly inside the Great Hall of the Ministry. Here the supposed leaders of the world, the hawks and doves of the World Council of Ministers, squawked and scrabbled to have their own way, unaware that *he*, Sir August, now controlled the planet.

"Pitiful," he spat, watching them, though it gave him no small pleasure to see what a lovely row he'd started. The idiots had played into his hands nicely. The global United Nations–like group was in full session, the ridiculous fools of the assembly arguing in amplified splendor round an enormous circular cherry table.

Sir August's gaze passed over them to the magnificent picture windows on the other side of the room, and through them to a panoramic view of London. Big Ben rose from near the Thames, an effective reminder, Sir August thought, of how little time they would have to meet his demands. Best of all, his clouds gathered ominously above, consolidating, growing darker and thicker with each passing moment. He himself had arranged for this particular display, knowing that masses of dark clouds, teamed with extreme cold, would connote impending doom. And rightly so.

Sir August bit into the lolly and turned his attention back to the ministers, watching with disdain. Their egos were so fragile that they would only meet at a round table. The only way they could see each other across the vast fifty-foot expanse of wood required to accommodate them all was via closed-circuit televisions, mounted in an outward-facing circle above the center of the table. It was the end of the first day of the conference, and tempers had frayed. They'd got absolutely nowhere; he'd been watching from the shadows ever since luncheon, when he'd disposed of the guards and other security staff.

"Poor babies," Sir August mumbled through his ice cream. Ties undone and scarves drooping, the pitiful figureheads slumped in discouragement. The only exceptions were the two ministers grandstanding at the moment.

Ah, well, he told himself, licking a drip off the bottom of his ice cream. Soon these poor idiots would be deposed—for all intents and purposes—and someone really intelligent would be running the show. He smiled.

A corpulent minister with an indistinguishable foreign accent and a sweaty face banged his fist on the polished cherry wood of the table. He boomed into his microphone, "These changes in weather are controlled and aggressive. We must respond with *force!*"

Across the room, another minister shook her head. She boomed with equal volume, "You disregard the fact that we came here to inaugurate a defense treaty!"

The man next to her erupted. "And *you* disregard the fact that these secret tests are already hostile!"

"I have said repeatedly," the woman began, through clenched teeth, "that those tests . . ."

"I can't bear it any longer," Sir August mumbled, dropping his ice-cream stick into a rubbish bin next to him. It clattered to the bottom of the bin, but no one heard over the ministers' voices.

He picked up his staff from where it leaned against the wall next to him and strode to the edge of the round table. *"Enough!"* he roared. His voice, without a microphone, was louder than all of the ministers' amplified voices combined, he noticed with satisfaction. And he was certain he made an impressive figure in his full Scottish regalia. Family tartan mantel draped over his shoulder, sporran hanging over his kilt close to his vital parts, he was utterly in command. Now, to reveal his power . . .

He slammed his staff on the table once, hard, for attention. In the cavernous room, the effect was similar to a gunshot. The ministers nearest him recoiled at the sudden, resounding noise, then gazed in awe at the dent he had made in the table with his staff. In one powerful leap, Sir August was atop the table, commanding the attention of the assembly. Treading on the ministers' agendas with deliberate disregard, he pointed to the sky with his staff.

"Now is the winter of your discontent . . ." His voice boomed round the room in the silence, and he thought how very like a Shakespearean actor he must look. He paused for maximum effect in his oration, holding the staff high. "Above you, the weather is changing. The temperature is dropping."

Openmouthed in shock, the hawkish minister breathed out, and his breath froze in a small white cloud.

"Soon it will be freezing." With his staff, Sir August reached down and snapped the gaping minister's mouth shut. "Why? Hmmm? *Why?*" He looked round the massive table for an answer.

None came.

Disappointed, he rolled his eyes and spoke in a voice one might use with a dim-witted child. "Because the weather, obviously, is no longer in God's hands." A slow smile spread over his face. "It's in mine."

"Impossible!" the minister at his feet cried out.

"Preposterous!" another screamed.

General chaos erupted, with all of the ministers objecting strenuously to Sir August's words. They stood; they banged on the table in pompous anger; their voices mingled and rose until they sounded like a playground full of children.

But Sir August talked over them, striding through the center of the table. "Those clouds," he shouted, pointing out the giant picture windows on the wall opposite with his staff, "all controlled by me, are creating the weather."

He paused to gaze at the clouds gathering ominously over the Thames. "This is merely the beginning," he said, over the murmurs and shouts of disgruntled ministers. "I have set in motion a chain reaction that will paralyze and ultimately destroy the city. The countdown has begun."

That silenced them. At last they stood quietly, staring at the clouds, stunned at the realization that the world was at his mercy. *They should be grateful,* Sir August thought. They came together to discuss problematic changes in the weather, and I am here to offer a solution.

He smiled round at them pleasantly. They looked frightened. Good, he thought. They should be. "My terms are simple. One billion. In gold. Or else. Shall we discuss?"

The room exploded in an uproar as first one minister, then another stood and shouted.

"Blackmail!"

"Outrage!"

"Get him out!"

"Terrorist!"

"Crazy!"

"Unacceptable!"

Sir August raised his staff. "Oh, *do* be quiet." He began conducting them as if they were musicians in an orchestra, which was not far from the truth. They were, in fact, essential to the execution of the glorious symphony that was the culmination of his dreams. Whenever a minister popped up to grandstand, Sir August waved his hand and his staff at him in the conductor's classic "shhhhh," as if to hush violins overwhelming a piano soloist's concerto.

"Hundreds of millions will die," he intoned, conducting them into silence. "They will freeze, drown, burn. Ice, snow, sun, rain—all at my disposal. Under my control." He smiled modestly. "You and your governments have no choice. You *will* buy your weather from me. Oh, yes. And, by God"—he wasn't joking—"you'll pay."

A few cocky ministers were slow to grasp the situation. They jumped to their feet and shouted their rejection of Sir August and his plot. *Oh well,* Sir August thought. He could afford to be patient for a moment or two more. There were a few slow children in every class.

"This is totally unacceptable. . . ."

"We won't yield to a madman!"

"Suit yourself," Sir August said cheerfully, hopping off the table. "As you wish." He crossed the room, ready to step out the door. *Fools,* he thought. But he had expected to have to provide some sort of demonstration. Well, they would get it.

He stood over a huge ornamental globe by the door, gripping his staff like a golf club, imagining it to be his Big Bertha driver. He shuffled his feet as golfers do until the spacing between his body and the globe was perfect, then stepped back for a practice swing. Lifting the club high over his right shoulder, he pulled through with his left arm, feeling his hips rotate as he executed the perfect swing. He'd learned it long ago from watching the world's best play at the ancient and royal course of St. Andrews.

Stepping forward again to the globe, he said thoughtfully, "Better enjoy it while you can." He placed the staff against the globe, ready to swing. He looked over at the table of stunned ministers and smiled. "You have until midnight tonight. Oh, by the way"—another toothy smile—"you have until midnight tonight."

After a smooth backswing, Sir August struck the globe cleanly. *Whack!* It rocketed, with profound symbolism, past the gobsmacked faces of the assembled ministers—making his point perfectly.

CHAPTER TWENTY

*Now would I give a thousand furlongs of sea for an
acre of barren ground, long heath, brown furze,
any thing. The wills above be done! but I would
fain die a dry death.*

The Tempest, *William Shakespeare*

Steed raced down the tunnel-like corridors that connected Colonel Invisible Jones's archives with the
rest of the Ministry. Making his way to the Ministry's
Psychiatric Operations Hospital, he prayed he wasn't
too late. He flew down the halls to the interrogation
cell block, to the end cell, where he knew Father liked
to place the worst offenders. He pressed the button,
opening the cell, but it was empty. Nothing at all
inside.

Time to get serious, Steed told himself. With new resolve to find Emma, he pressed a button on his watch.
Beep-beep-beep . . .

Good. The microtag was working. It wouldn't be
long now.

• • •

Emma didn't know that the homing device in her boot was leading Steed directly to her. She did, however, realize vaguely that Bad Emma was carrying her somewhere, with Father in the lead. She was so tired . . . woozy . . . one minute, aphrodisiac darts . . . the next, poisonous gas . . .

Bad Emma had stopped—at a window or a door, it seemed to Emma. There was more light. If she could just go to sleep . . .

But a door opened somewhere behind her in the Ministry corridor. Mother's voice sounded. "Sorry, Father. The game's up."

Bad Emma turned, still cradling her in her arms—though none too tenderly—and Emma, squinting, thought she saw a miniscule revolver in Mother's hand, aimed at Father.

Father seemed to sense the weapon. Oozing scorn, Father let it all out. "Careful with that, Mother. Might go off. Wouldn't want another accident, would we? Only half working, as you are." She stepped toward Mother. "Poor Mother. You finally figured it out—too late."

"Nonsense," Mother hissed. "Mother knows best. I want you to release Mrs. Peel."

"Certainly." Emma saw Father smile nastily. "But which one?"

Mother, startled, looked at one and then the other. Emma tried to wave at him, to say "Here I am," but her hand refused to obey. It hung limply over Bad Emma's arm.

Then all hell broke loose. Emma struggled to follow what happened next. As best she could tell with her head hanging next to Bad Emma, Father struck Mother, knocking his gun away. Mother retaliated, and they struggled like late-night wrestlers until Father pushed Mother over, out of his chair. Mother hit the ground with a groan, and writhed there as the chair circled round on automatic, out of Mother's reach. Father pushed Bad Emma through the door ahead of her, then followed them out. Emma heard Father say wryly, "It's really not Mother's day," as they stepped outside into some strange white stuff. It was falling all around them. . . .

Christmas already? Emma thought. It seemed St. Swithin's Day had only just come. Where did the time go . . .

The hawkish minister of the indeterminate accent, who was in fact from one of the newly independent countries of Eastern Europe, rushed to the door used by the mad golfer as he made his exit. Locked! The minister banged on the door with his fists. "Guards! Guards!" He used his most intimidating, blustering shout—the one that usually brought his assistants running with terror in their eyes.

There was no response. He imagined the paramilitary men outside lying bound and gagged on the floor—or, given the maniacal nature of the Scottish golfer, more probably dead. This was absurd—they were the leaders of the world, the masters of the universe! And they were locked in the room like a group of naughty toddlers!

But even as he turned angrily from the door and rushed to try the set of doors across the room, he knew it would be locked as well. How had the terrorist been allowed into the building in the first place? The man dressed as a swashbuckling Scot had given a whole new meaning to the American group of terrorists known as the Weathermen in the 1970s. He allowed a wry smile to curl up one side of his mouth. Such a wit he had. No wonder he, Sergei, had rocketed to stardom out of the masses.

Someone would pay for this; he would see to it. To make *them,* the most powerful people in the world, look like fools!

Damnation! The other door was locked as well. He yanked powerfully at the French door handles, aware that others were watching him, *Such a hero, that Sergei Ivanovich.* . . . Panting from the unusual exertion, the minister ran to the telephone by the wall with all the panache of an American action hero about to save them all. The guards had carefully labeled and checked all their cell phones at the door; it had been agreed that private phone calls would be intrusive and disrespectful in the midst of their critical meeting. He picked up the receiver, but heard no tone. Dead.

As he slowly replaced the receiver, in stunned disbelief that this could happen in what was very nearly the twenty-first century, he momentarily forgot his show of strength and bluster for the other ministers. He thought instead of his image at home. His country was struggling through the post-honeymoon period of independence and economic decentralization, and people were already growing edgy with the lack of improvement in their standard of living. They were learning the hard way that the free market system was purchased with a price. Over these last few months, he'd often felt he was hanging on by his fingernails, barely maintaining control. He'd heard the thinly veiled contempt in his people's comments, even among those who worked for him.

Sergei had come to this conference knowing that it was a watershed: he had to grasp leadership, show his people and the world that their little nation was a power to be reckoned with. If he failed to handle this situation well, there would be hell to pay. They might even kill him. It had happened to others before him.

He heard a wave of sound, a cross between a gasp and a sigh, and turned to see the other ministers moving slowly toward the picture window. And with good reason. The mother of all blizzards had begun to rage outside, walls of the white stuff blowing in a nasty gale. And the snow was already accumulating, rather than

melting on the pavements as one would expect. That
meant the temperature had been lowered to a dangerous
degree.

The madman had been deadly serious. As Sergei
crossed to the window and stared out as if in a trance,
he knew that they had made a terrible error in under-
estimating the golfer. And he also knew that his future
was very bleak indeed. He would be fortunate to be ex-
iled to a place as cold and snowy as London looked at
the moment—perhaps the steppe of Outer Siberia, if
they didn't kill him first.

By the time Steed got there, Emma was gone again. The
alarm siren sounded urgently throughout the Ministry,
compounding his sense of disaster.

He raced down the corridor, to where Mother lay injured on the floor.

"The roof, Steed. The roof!!" Mother's voice was
wracked with pain.

Steed raced off again, umbrella in hand, bowler
firmly in place against the weather. Climbing the stairs
three at a time, he hoped he wasn't too late. "In the
name of Saint Swithin, let her be all right," he panted as
he ascended all of six flights. Over the years, he'd
learned it was faster than waiting for the lifts.

At last he emerged, gasping for breath, onto the Ministry roof. It was dark, snowing heavily, and freezing
cold. A cruel wind blew the snow at high speed, stinging
his face. He staggered to a stop, staring out across the
rooftop.

In the distance, far away across the roof, he squinted
at an odd-looking apparition through the blizzard.
What . . . ? Looming from the fog and snow, a vast
onionlike shape, apparently made of silk, billowed in
the air like some Jules Verne monster. Staring, he recognized gas cells and tanks of liquid oxygen . . . and then

the penny dropped. It was a souped-up, high-tech meteorological balloon. Another appropriation from Prospero, no doubt. Steed raced toward it with abandon.

As he neared, he saw Father in the cockpit, ready to escape. She heard him approaching at a run, and shouted, "Better luck next time, Steed!" as, with a hiss of air, the balloon lifted off with impressive speed. He lunged for it, his fingertips nearly brushing the glowing silk, but it was just out of his reach. Damn! And Emma was almost certainly on that balloon somewhere. . . .

He raced to the edge of the roof, but found no exit there. Hurrying to the fire escape, he clambered down its icy steps, hanging out over the street five levels up. Heights had never been his specialty in agent training . . . but this was no time to freeze. Steed put his umbrella in his teeth and climbed down toward street level, step by icy step.

As Bad Emma swung her through the door, the cold air hit Emma like a slap. She felt her mind clearing, knew she had to take action. Up ahead, she saw a huge white balloon, like a weather balloon, with flames shooting from its burner.

Bad Emma began to run toward the balloon, still carrying her. *Carpe diem,* she told herself, and kicked her legs down, out of Bad Emma's grasp. Then she twisted round and delivered a hefty karate chop to her namesake's neck. Bad Emma reeled, staggering away from her, but Emma could see she was aching for revenge. Emma had barely regained her own balance when she saw Bad Emma execute an impressive flip, aiming for her with those huge feet. Did her own feet look that big, or was that some modification—an improvement on the original—by Sir August? She couldn't help but wonder.

Emma, her reflexes slowed by Father's noxious gas attack in the cell, didn't react until it was too late. The impact caught her squarely under the chin, knocking her backward toward the edge of the roof.

Not again! Emma thought, as Bad Emma pinned her to the snowy, slippery roof, her head and shoulders hanging out over Horseguards Avenue. *Pity there's no time to enjoy the view,* Emma thought, before she began to struggle in earnest.

She pummelled the bionic woman with her hands, but Bad Emma withstood them effortlessly. *More,* Emma thought. *I've got to have more. . . .*

She twisted her neck until she was within biting range of Bad Emma's arm, the one pinning her to the roof. She sank her teeth in, but withdrew when she hit metal. *Yecchhhh,* she thought. *Won't try that again on a half-bionic clone.*

Seriously worried, gasping for breath, Emma rallied herself for the big kick. One . . . two . . . three . . . she coiled her legs up, brought them round Bad Emma's muscular sides, and kicked with all her might against Bad Emma's torso. It worked. Bad Emma hadn't been expecting her to retaliate so effectively, and went hurtling backward onto the drifting rooftop.

But Bad Emma was a fighting machine. And she was just human enough to be really angry now, Emma saw. Her eyes glinted with the eerie menace Emma had seen before. Far too often, in fact.

Emma moved away from the edge of the roof as she saw Bad Emma accelerate toward her with disturbing speed. Emma dodged one kick to her head, then took one to the solar plexus. Stumbling, gasping, she parried as best she could, until Bad Emma delivered a really nasty kick to her leg. She crumpled, sinking onto the rooftop. Emma felt her evil twin seize her in a deadly embrace, expelling what breath she had managed to take in.

"Ooooof!" Half expecting to be squeezed to death, as if by boa constrictor, Emma steeled herself for the worst. She was surprised when Bad Emma suddenly tucked her under one arm and ran with abandon for the weather balloon, apparently not slowed in the least by her cargo. A ladder dangled dangerously, hanging fifty feet below the balloon.

No, Emma thought. *Surely not.* As she twisted round to see, Father began to reel in the ladder, shooting flaming gas into the balloon.

At last, Steed thought, stepping off the last step of the blasted fire escape onto terra firma. Plucking the umbrella out of his mouth with frozen fingers, he worked his jaws. "Thank God that bit's over," he murmured, and looked up at the ghostly balloon.

"Good heavens!" he cried, a bit disturbed at the sight of two tiny Emmas dangling from what appeared to be a thread attached to the balloon. The ladder was being coiled up into the balloon. Had he only *stayed* on the blasted roof . . .

As the balloon drifted over the city, Steed followed beneath it at a run, plunging through snowdrifts with no regard whatsoever for his shoes. It was the first time he had ever done so. Trubshaw would not approve.

In the sky over London, Emma was hoisted up into the balloon—effortlessly, from all appearances—by Bad Emma. Inside the balloon at last, struggling, Emma wrested herself free from the woman's bodyhold. Flames blazed next to them, feeding the balloon its breath of hot air. The white fabric of the balloon billowed around them, as if they were in a giant cloud. *Definitely cumulus*, Emma thought, before Bad Emma pounced, catching Emma in a viselike grip.

Emma pushed against her nemesis with all she had; still, Bad Emma was forcing her closer and closer to the flames. Struggling mightily, she felt the heat of the flames on the back of her head, wondered if her hair had caught fire. . . .

Aaargh! Emma won a few inches' reprieve, but knew she had to do better. Frantically, she took one hand off Bad Emma and grappled around behind her back for the gas supply lever. She'd seen it a few moments ago. . . . Fluttering, her hand found it, and flipped the lever.

Whhooooooooosh! Gas flew from the tank, and Emma knew she had probably sealed her own doom. But at least she would have rid the earth of two unconscionable villains.

"You *fool!*" Father screamed, turning from the controls. She simmered with fury, perceiving that the balloon had begun to deflate.

Looking at the canister, Emma saw a label: "Liquid Oxygen—Dangerous." The needle on the canister's pressure gauge climbed steadily as she watched, then quivered right off the scale to a red zone marked DANGER. She looked up, saw that they were losing height. Father started in her direction with fiendish intensity. Emma backed away slowly, resigning herself to the possibility that this might be the end.

CHAPTER TWENTY-ONE

Poor souls, they perish'd.
The Tempest, *William Shakespeare*

Steed watched from below, anguished, as the balloon
seemed to deflate, then lose direction roughly over
Scotland Yard. As he watched, it accelerated, though
how he couldn't guess. It flew into the driving blizzard
over the snow-covered city, high enough to clear the
buildings, but not, Steed saw with trepidation, high
enough to pass over a massive Wonderland Weather billboard in the Charing Cross Road.

"Of all the ironic twists," Steed snapped, heading for
the billboard on foot. Rapt, trotting beneath, he watched
as the balloon drifted closer and closer to the threatening billboard. Then he saw something far more frightening. Every muscle in his body tensed as he saw Father
and Emma struggling, Father trying to shove Emma
overboard.

He stopped and stood agape in the snow as Bad

Emma got into the action. He watched as she got underneath Emma, picked her up as if she were a mannequin, and simply . . . tossed her into space.

Steed's mouth fell open for the first time in his life. He ran, arms extended in a futile gesture as he looked up at Emma hurtling downward. He couldn't catch her, he *knew* he couldn't, yet he had to. . . . Out of the corner of his eye, he saw the electrics on the multicolored Wonderland Weather sign fizz and spark. "SOONER THAN YOU THINK!" the billboard screamed in tall orange letters.

Too true, Steed thought. *Too true.*

The balloon actually began to rise before it hit the billboard, but couldn't make it. He wasn't really watching, as he had his eye on Emma, but all of London couldn't help but see the huge fireball of liquid oxygen, gas, and electrics.

The city lit up, and Emma was caught in its glow, red in its reflection. She fell in slow motion, it seemed to Steed, limbs extended. Steed's face was a mask of dread as he watched. The last he saw of her, she was only slightly northeast of him, but he didn't know exactly where she'd fall. He watched until she disappeared, then his eyes snapped shut.

"Stiff upper lip, Steed," he reminded himself. Tears ran down his face anyway, and he set off immediately in pursuit. If by some miracle she were alive, he'd never let anything endanger her again. . . . As he hurried in the direction she'd fallen, he saw the burning balloon wreckage hanging like a defeated monster above him. Wires trailed from the billboard, sparks sputtered, and electrics spit as snow fell on them.

Then the sky lit up and he covered his ears as a huge secondary explosion ignited like a flash of fireworks, illuminating the Wonderland Weather slogan for the last time. He was so close that the hot blast of the shock wave knocked him to the ground, against a rubbish bin.

Steed struggled to his feet and plunged on through the deep snow at a run, holding his watch with the receiver for Emma's microtag in his hand. It directed him toward Trafalgar Square. An overturned double-decker bus blocked his way from Charing Cross; he clambered over it, slid down the other side. He fought his way through the snow into an empty Trafalgar Square. No Emma.

Looking about desperately, he saw only Nelson's column shooting up to the sky, and the lion statues. But wait—the beeping had accelerated when he walked toward the lions. He couldn't see her, but she was close by. He half dreaded finding her crumpled body, but knew he must go to her.

Stepping forward toward the giant snowdrifts that surrounded the lion statues, Steed saw a familiar figure cradled in the paws of one of the beasts. The outstretched paws of the lion had collected several feet of snow, which had made a bed for Emma. Lunging toward her, he gave a cry as he saw her limbs outstretched, face white with cold and death, gone forever . . . lost to the snow.

As he reached for her, he saw her eyes flicker. She smiled and looked right at him. "Prince Charming, I presume." She sounded just the slightest bit shaky, and he didn't trust his voice to reply as he gently picked her up and carried her safely down to the ground.

Steed cleared his throat and brushed some—er—melted snow off his cheeks. "Hardly," he said, looking into her eyes. "A microtag concealed in your boots, Mrs. Peel."

"Thank you, Trubshaw."

Steed fussed over Emma, dusting the snow off, rubbing her arms to get her warm.

"How do you feel?" he asked, concerned.

"No broken bones," she said lightly, though he noticed she favored one leg. He eyed it suspiciously.

"And the *other* Mrs. Peel?" He almost wished he hadn't thought of it. Suddenly he looked at her with veiled suspicion. Was this really his Emma? He studied her eyes carefully, saw the dancing spark of warmth and humor he'd come to rely upon.

"Dispatched, I think," she said. "Sad, in a way . . ."

"Hmmm. I wonder."

They walked on, determined to get out of the snowy night. They'd both been shivering for a good long time. But Steed couldn't resist looking at Emma, wondering . . .

"Yes?" Emma finally asked, stopping short.

"I can't quite get her out of my head," he said apologetically. "I was just thinking. . . ." Without warning, which was half the battle in these situations, he thought, he pulled her toward him and kissed her full on the lips. As the snow continued to fall, they remained locked together, well and truly snogging. They savored it, indulging themselves, unable to help it—until Steed pulled away.

Emma stared at him. "Unless I'm very much mistaken, that was a kiss, Steed."

"Yes . . . technically."

" 'Technically'?"

"Mrs. Peel, I'm surprised at you. Surely you realize that I would *never* presume . . . More in the spirit of scientific inquiry. Hard evidence, you might say."

"Mmm. I realized that, immediately."

"Of course you did. I needed proof you were really Mrs. Peel."

Emma nodded reasonably. "I see. And . . . convinced?"

"Still thinking . . ." He looked at her out of the corner of his eye as they walked.

"What are you thinking?"

"That I need to keep a stiff upper lip."

Emma linked her arm through his as they set off through the blizzard, out of Trafalgar Square towards Whitehall and the Ministry.

•   •   •

Sergei stared out the picture window, rapt by the disaster that they had allowed to befall the entire world. All of the ministers had remained glued to the window, watching the unbelievable sight of London paralyzed by the sort of snowfall normally reserved for high mountain passes. Many of the ministers were shivering with the cold; there was no one to adjust the temperature of the great hall.

For once, Sergei was glad he had his massive fat reserves. The lessons of his people throughout countless famines had served him well. But he was beginning to long for a drink—he could use a Stoli round about now. It had been hours since his prebreakfast pick-me-up.

He stood at the front of the crowd, feeling the cold come through the window. The red buses that had stopped operating earlier that day were now buried in snow, which was still accumulating at a frightening rate. He suspected that even the door to the Ministry building had to be snowed in by now. The streets were utterly paralyzed; emergency vehicles were useless. If one of them were to suffer a heart attack from the strain, there would be no ambulance.

A feeling of powerlessness overtook him. He was hobbled here by the civility of the English; normally, at home, he carried a weapon at all times. If only he had his pistol here, he could have shot through the door long ago and got help—saved them all. Now they were stuck here for the duration. And no one seemed to realize they were stranded. . . .

Brenda always felt a thrill when Mother spoke to the PM on the hotline. And Downing Street was just a few streets away . . . at moments like this she felt she could practically reach out and touch him. Brenda tended the other telephones while keeping one ear tuned to their conversation through Mother's open door.

Mother said, "Yes, I know, sir. The city is paralyzed. Held hostage. Yes, sir, we have. There's a dense cloud formation moving northeast, sir. Some sort of radio transmitter."

Brenda waited while the PM spoke, and sighed as she thought of John. She hoped he was all right . . . oh, for the day when he would walk in and sweep her off her feet! *Well, it could happen,* she told herself.

"Of course we have it under control, sir. . . ." Mother listened again for a moment, squirming. "Well, not *quite* under control, but . . ." He rubbed his eyes with his free hand. "Yes, sir. I understand, sir. Our agents are on the case right now. . . . Two of them, sir. A man . . . and a woman, sir."

After he'd rung off, Brenda carried the milky, sugary tea in to Mother. She didn't speak to him, taking her cue from the way he was holding his head in his hands. She set down the steaming National Trust pottery mug with the quote from Winston Churchill on it—"A day spent away from Chartwell is a day wasted"—and left quietly.

Snow continued to fall mercilessly over London. The city was clogged and choked with it. Even Buckingham Palace was snowed in. But not far from the palace, where the Queen was snowed into enforced residence, was a mysterious anomaly: the Serpentine Island. The lazy boating lake in the middle of Hyde Park was unfrozen around the island, and the island itself was utterly snowless. In fact, it looked more like a tropical jungle. Heavy undergrowth had sprung up in response to a steamy cluster of microclimates hovering over the island alone.

But that wasn't the only unusual thing about Serpentine Island that night. If it hadn't been dark, and the boathouse and the restaurant hadn't been closed, and if everyone hadn't been inside trying to stay warm, boaters would have been stunned by what came floating out of the water. "Alien sightings on Serpentine!" the forty-eight point heading on the *News Express* would have screamed.

For two inhuman white pods floated along in the icy water. In the misty fog and tumbling snowflakes, they slowly bubbled and floated ever closer to the island. The perfect white spheres might have indicated that the beings were from a superior civilization.

When at last they hit the shore, any observers would have seen that the spheres were, in fact, human-sized. The immaculate surface of the bubbles perforated; slits appeared. Then, incredibly, the beings seemed to hatch out of the eggs. From inside, there was the sound of unzipping zippers, and the eggs peeled away to reveal—a decidedly superior civilization.

For the inhabitants, Emma Peel and John Steed, were British.

Despite their superior intelligence, they did not know that deep in the interior of the dark island, a mechanical peacock had spread its tail and was photographing their every move.

"A walk in the park?" Steed asked Mrs. Peel. Looking at him, Emma saw that he was resplendent in a freshly pressed suit, the inevitable bowler and umbrella, and—because he was happy, he said—a red rose in his lapel.

"How lovely," she responded. Less traditionally attired in one of her favorite black leather catsuits and the Trubshaw boots, Emma was ready for action. There was no time to lose.

Steed pulled the BROLLY map from an inside jacket pocket. "An island in the Serpentine," he sighed. "According to Colonel Jones, this is a map of a secret Ministry installation. Sold off years ago to—"

"Wonderland Weather, I'd bet."

"Quite." Steed straightened his lapels, adjusting the rose.

Emma watched him, incredulous. How *could* he fuss so with his clothing? "I really think we should go. Do you mind?"

He gave her a distracted smile. "No, not at all, Mrs. Peel." He punched the tip of his umbrella into each white pod; they deflated cooperatively into little white heaps of fabric on the ground. "After you."

"No, after you."

Like Livingstone and Stanley, they crept through the thick jungle undergrowth, threading through tangled creepers and vines. Wind from the continuing blizzard could be felt on the island, though it was a warm zephyr in the tropical microclimate. It moved the lush vegetation in frightening bursts, creating flitting shadows. More than once, Emma felt they were not alone.

"A fine time for a walk in the woods." Emma saw Steed stop suddenly, then duck behind a tall shrub. She followed suit.

"Something up ahead," he whispered. "How are you with animals?"

"Two-legged or four-legged?"

"I wish I knew."

Sensing something just ahead, Steed and Emma inched forward carefully. At last Emma parted the branches and vines to reveal a six-foot-tall pink teddy bear, motionless. Knowing Sir August, the teddy was likely to be dead. Rushing to the bear, Steed knelt at its side as Emma slipped off the plush pink head.

"Alas, poor teddy," Steed said.

"I knew him, Steed." Emma looked at the man's face. "Penrose . . . in charge of antimatter fission on Prospero."

"The teddy bears must be having a picnic. We're getting warm, Mrs. Peel."

Emma and Steed pushed on through the forest. Steed said, "I say, I don't much like the feel of this."

"I know what you mean," Emma said. She had an ominous feeling, a sense of evil afoot. . . .

They parted the trees to see not one, but two more bears. Turquoise and lilac. Dead. Emma huddled over the furry corpses, lifting their masks as Steed stood watch. All round them, the forest shimmered eerily, and the wind in the trees produced strange harmonic chords.

"Professor Pemberton," Emma said. "And Dr. Nesbitt. Trail's growing very warm indeed."

"And warmer still, Mrs. Peel. 'O brave new world that has such people in it. . . .' "

Steed indicated the woods ahead, as if he knew what was there. Emma turned and saw a trail of teddy bear corpses.

"Hmm—a little *too* warm." Emma separated from Steed to investigate the trail. Green, scarlet, mauve . . . such an immense loss for the scientific community, she thought. A tragedy. She knelt to take the head off the bear closest to her, then glimpsed something through the trees, not far away. Hearing a noise, she stood, then wheeled to face a most disturbing development.

The razor-sharp, pointed blade of a familiar silver staff pricked at her throat. As clouds scudded clear of the moon, she saw—his mad eyes gleaming from the string of teddy bear executions—Sir August de Wynter.

"Sssssshhhhh." He held his blade against her throat, so she could feel the pricking of it. "I could snuff you out in a moment."

Emma felt a nasty urge to taunt him. "Really? What a surprise. Always trouble at the teddy bears' picnic . . . I should have known." She smiled. "Shall we dance?"

"No," he growled. "Not now. Too late for that."

"Really?" she asked, surprised. "I thought you liked to dance. How could you forget? 'August was a lovely month, lovely as can be. Now it's turned to winter, cold as cold can . . .' "

Defiant, Emma grabbed for the staff, but Sir August blocked her, putting his staff across the small of her back and pulling her up against him, until they were eye to eye.

"Foolish girl," he said. "Look"—he caught a stray snowflake in his hand and held it up for her to see. It was perfect, lovely in its symmetry and complexity.

"So beautiful, so deadly. This blizzard shall be your tomb. What coffin could be more exquisite?" He blew the snowflake at her. "Any final requests?"

She narrowed her eyes at him. "Now that you ask, there was one thing I wanted to clear up. . . ." She knew that *he* knew she was asking about their little tryst in the mirrored chamber. It had bothered her every time she took off and put on a catsuit; for when she'd come around from the love potion on the velvet divan, her suit had been unzipped to the fullest extent. She needed to know if she'd been compromised.

"That?" he asked, momentarily off guard. Then she saw his face go deliberately expressionless. *Of course,* Emma thought. *He knows he has that power over me.* As she watched, fury suffused him. He brought the blade around, pressing it against her cheek. She could feel the sharp tip. *Well, well,* she thought. *He's angry about something. I'll bet he never got to . . .*

She turned her head away from the razor-sharp point and saw his resolution waver. Then she saw an idea dawn in his dangerously psychotic eyes; she could read it. He would not kill her; he would let her live in torment, never knowing exactly what had happened that day. She would wonder forever.

"Emma, dearest . . ." He laughed a short laugh. "You'll never know."

She heard a swishing noise through the leaves as he released her. She wheeled; he was gone. Vanished. How did he manage to disappear like that? As she searched for him in vain through the mist, she saw Steed looming out of the darkness.

To her great satisfaction, he said the words she'd longed to hear. "You're needed, Mrs. Peel."

CHAPTER TWENTY-TWO

*Jove's lightning, the precursors o' th' dreadful
thunderclaps . . . the fire and cracks of sulphurous
roaring . . .*

The Tempest, *William Shakespeare*

Steed ushered Emma into the phone box at the
exact center of the island, then squeezed in beside
her. He smelled her hair—she used some sort of
herbal shampoo—and the leather of the catsuit. The suit
was so voluptuous, so enticing . . . he marveled that she
could walk the streets of London in it without being
mobbed. He hoped some day he would have the chance
to run his hands along the entire stretch of her long leg,
from Trubshaw boot toe to inner thigh, to the seam
where . . .

He saw her eyeing him as she picked up the phone.
"Excuse me," he said, hoping he sounded perfectly composed. "Equipment needs adjusting."

"Nothing broken, I hope?" she asked, teasing him.
She could be relentless, he thought.

Fiddling with his umbrella in front of him, he said, by

way of excuse, "My *umbrella*, Mrs. Peel. Tight fit in here."

"Allow me," Emma said. Steed felt a moment of delighted panic as he wondered exactly what she was offering to do, then heard her speak into the receiver. "How now brown cow? The quick brown fox jumped over the lazy dog." She pressed the 'B' button, and the floor began to lower. They rode down together. Steed longed for the ride to go on, and on, and on. He wasn't particularly keen to enter the headquarters of the sinister BROLLY, not when he could enjoy the proximity of Mrs. Peel. Who knew what awaited them below?

They emerged from the darkness, poised for action, into a bright, empty white space. The ceiling was so low that the top of Steed's bowler barely cleared it. The place was utterly deserted, devoid of alarms and everything else. Steed frowned at Emma, hearing only the sound of his shoes on the floor as he led the way into a hall. Emma followed, her boots also tapping on the smooth white surface.

Steed stopped in midstep, motioned for her to stop. They listened: complete silence. *Tap-tap-tap,* their shoes sounded as they started forward again. They exchanged wary glances as the perspective changed. Not unlike Hallucinogen Hall, Steed thought. They stepped into an area that had the appearance of an immense, neoclassical car park. Empty. White. *Rather enigmatic,* Steed thought. *Definitely forbidding.*

Up ahead, they saw a pillar supporting a claustrophobic passageway. *Tap-tap-tap* . . . the echoing of their shoes against the floor remained the only sound. Until suddenly, a phone rang out of nowhere, startling both of them with its brisk double ring. Steed stepped round, looking for the phone, joined by Emma, and found the perspective changed yet again. *Definitely Hallucinogen Hall in the city,* Steed thought.

Now, ahead of them stretched a line of immaculate

Doric columns, carrying on to the vanishing point down a narrow passageway. The ceiling was disturbingly low; Steed found it uncomfortably oppressive. He thought he sensed that Emma, by his side, was equally uncomfortable in the cramped space.

Somewhere, the phone continued to ring, echoing hollowly in the low-ceilinged hallway. Steed searched with Emma, around and behind pillar after pillar, until behind one of them Steed saw an old Bakelite phone. He picked up.

"Hello? Hello?" As he listened, the line went dead. Emma watched him put down the phone and walk on, as if he'd just called the speaking clock. "Wrong number," he said over his shoulder.

They headed off down the vast promenade, their footsteps echoing in the cavernous space. Steed took pleasure in walking next to Emma in companionable silence, as if they'd known each other forever. Sometimes, he felt they had. She was everything he had ever imagined a woman might be, and more. The number of nights he'd dreamed of her, not knowing her face or her name, but her fearless nature . . . It wouldn't do to let on, though. He carefully kept his gaze straight ahead, his eyes averted.

Steed saw, in the distance, what appeared to be a window . . . a wall of glass. He and Emma moved closer, and saw that as they approached, it grew larger. *Wait*, Steed thought. Not one, but two . . . three . . . no, a whole *structure* of glass. They turned a corner, and Steed was grateful to have reached the end of the promenade.

It was not a window at all, nor even a series of them, that stood before them. It was a huge glass dome that filled a high space, yet another huge white room—this time with a very high ceiling indeed. Steed and Emma stepped up to look it over. He couldn't quite tell what lay beyond the dome, but Steed noted its pitch was gentle enough that they could walk over it.

"Should lead to the control module," Emma whispered. "Antimatter circuits will be close by."

"I wouldn't know where to start," Steed said, gazing around him as if lost. "You make it sound so simple."

Emma tossed him a superior look over her shoulder. "I did design it, after all."

Ah, right, Steed thought. *Point taken.* Salvaging what remained of his self-respect, he led the way onto the surface of the dome, stepping carefully on the glass. Their footsteps were louder yet on the crystalline surface. They continued up the dome to its center, and when they looked down through the glass they saw, hundreds of yards below, a control room housing a huge glass bubble. Emma sank down first to her knees to see better, then spread-eagled herself on the dome to gaze directly down on the bubble. Steed, tucking his umbrella under his arm, did the same.

"Good Lord," Emma said, impressed. "It's ten times the size of the one we used for research at Prospero."

To one side of the giant bubble they saw a vertical tower, sturdily built of welded steel, like an offshore oil rig. A steel catwalk connected a miniature version of the glass bubble, placed halfway up the tower, to its parent. Around the tower, storm patterns fizzed and crackled, and black clouds spit rain. It might have been floating in the middle of the North Sea, for all the good being indoors did it.

"As you were saying, Mrs. Peel."

"Hmm. A bit larger than I remember."

"Anything else you'd care to mention—strictly from the expert's point of view?"

She nodded. "Just one thing. Soon the process will be irreversible. We have a few minutes before it blows."

"How comforting. I'll stop Sir August, you disarm the antimatter circuits—"

"If I can find them."

From afar, beneath them, they heard a deep rumbling. Considering their present position, it wasn't a good sign.

"Your confidence is inspiring," he said ironically.

"Feeling's mutual. Shall we?"

They *tick-tack*ed their way off the glass dome with care, hearing a slow, deep growl. They looked at each other. The growl increased in volume and seismic intensity until the floor began to vibrate. Then, on top of that, a distant engine noise revved up, and electric current began to hum, growing to a deafening buzz. Instinctively, they flinched from not only the volume but the sound of raw voltage. Something extremely powerful had been set in motion.

Time for action. Near a pillar next to the dome Steed saw an open staircase leading downward. It had to lead to the control module.

"This way," he called. Emma followed him toward the staircase as both the rumble and the roar grew, persuading them beyond doubt that whatever climax they were building toward was fast approaching.

In the lower, smaller glass sphere, Sir August sat in the hot seat, controlling the storms. The fizz and crackle of the minor storms Steed and Emma had seen were just background noise to him. Smiling nonchalantly, he flipped a switch with a flourish, unleashing a cyclone. On an array of monitors above him, he saw with satisfaction that the blizzard continued to paralyze the city.

He particularly enjoyed the monitor that showed Big Ben and another that displayed Buckingham Palace. Big Ben, one of London's greatest landmarks, was now so caked with blowing, wet snow as to be useless. Staring at the monitor, he gloated. He'd purposely added just enough moisture to the snow to make sure it would stick to everything. Much messier; far more overwhelming for both people and machines.

"Antimatter fission starts now. Five minutes and counting . . ." The woman's voice over the loudspeaker had been synthesized to resemble Emma's. He loved hearing it, so even though there were no longer any BROLLY scientists alive to hear the announcements—how he'd enjoyed disposing of those potential traitors once they'd fulfilled their purpose—he let them resound throughout BROLLY headquarters.

Red numbers flew backward on his display as the Emma-like synthesized voice began a countdown. "Four minutes, fifty-eight seconds. Four minutes, fifty-six seconds . . ." Sir August had his trusty wind-up clock nearby; it, too, was ticking cheerfully toward the countdown. He'd had to switch from his teddy to the clock at the tender age of seven, upon leaving for public school. But he'd never been able to wean himself from *it*. Now, even as master of the world, he needed the clock. He picked it up and held it to his ear, as he had all those nights at school when he'd been so lonely.

Checking the monitors, Sir August saw that from the distance, the dark clouds he'd specified were sweeping in most satisfactorily. In fact, he thought they looked a bit like an army, marching into London, spreading shadows through the streets. For the storm could not be allowed to flag. This was only the beginning. They'd see. He watched the fast-moving black clouds for a moment, gloating. Unnatural energy crackled and flashed deep within them, discharging minor voltages, but saving themselves for the big moment—which he, Prospero, controlled!

He'd seen Steed and Emma, little Xs lying on the high glass of the ceiling dome, peering down on his domain. But they couldn't stop him now. Nothing could. Pity she'd have to suffer so, but still . . . he *had* given her the choice. Quite generous of him, really.

He sighed. It was a glorious night indeed, the culmination of all his life's work and his fondest dreams.

Steed and Emma closed the door behind them as they entered the control room. They clambered into the vertical tower, where Emma said, "Look! The circuit layout. Handy, this . . ." She studied the wall-mounted chart briefly, then said, "Come on—into the Weather Tube. We haven't long now." She led the way down some stairs, which led to more stairs, which spiraled tightly downward into infinity.

As Steed and Emma descended, they heard a tremendous noise. Steed felt the hair on his hands rising with static electricity; saw Emma's hair rising ahead of him. Around them, the walls shook with the force of an almighty engine. Inside the tube, frost formed. The air grew colder by the second. As they stepped down, down, and still farther down, snowflakes began to fall. The temperature plummeted disastrously. Steed began to lose feeling in his fingers and knew that Emma must be freezing too. Wind buffeted them with remarkable force, slamming what felt like walls of frigid air against them.

Emma turned to look at him, hanging onto the railing with both hands, and yelled up at him to make herself heard. "Must be a hatch somewhere! I need to locate the circuits, break the codes, disconnect the wires."

"How will you know if it works?" he shouted down.

"I won't—until I make the right connection. Better keep your head down. . . ."

"So much for science," Steed shouted dismissively. "I'll stick to swordplay."

A roaring blizzard came at them now, snow and ice added to the cold and wind. Steed and Emma pushed on, slowly freezing, persevering against all odds. This was what their training had prepared them for. As Steed watched Emma below him, he thought again that she was a woman to be treasured. He could not imagine another woman capable of carrying on in adversity the way she did. And he knew firsthand from testing her identity after she'd fallen from the balloon that she was well practiced in keeping *her* upper lip stiff.

They were midway down the staircase. Emma hung onto the stair rail in the howling gale with one hand, pointing at something with the other. Steed looked, and through the flying snow saw a hatch. "Just what I've been looking for," she shouted. "This will lead toward the junction tube." Emma turned a wheeled door, and he moved closer to her so he could hear. "Go down," she shouted. "Don't wait for me."

"Perish the thought." Then, as she turned to go, he couldn't resist saying, "Oh, just in case . . ."

She twisted round again to look at him. "Good luck?"

"Something like that. Not that you need it, of course."

She looked at him strangely for a moment; almost as if she were gloating, Steed thought. Then she called to him, "You might need it more than me."

Steed gave her a long, lingering look as she disappeared through the hatch. He felt a sudden breeze as Emma's door slammed shut. Looking down the tube, he saw a most remarkable sight, and knew what Emma had meant: a spinning column of air, not unlike the photos he'd seen of tornadoes, but without the debris, was coming straight toward him.

CHAPTER TWENTY-THREE

*He'll be hanged yet, though every drop of water
swear against it and gape at wid'st to glut him.*
The Tempest, *William Shakespeare*

The Queen mourned this latest terrorist attack on London, though to her knowledge, no one had died in the blizzard—yet. She sat next to the Queen Mother and watched BBC1, which had gone to continuous news. She could see the strain on the two newscasters who'd been stuck in the recording studio all day.

"It is a dark day indeed for England," the red-faced male announcer proclaimed. Why did they always have to be so dramatic? the Queen wondered. Why couldn't the man just get on with it? "London and the Home Counties are paralyzed under five feet of snow." Remote cameras fed footage of the ruined, deserted city to the central studio, and the Queen stared now at the awe-inspiring images before her. Saint Paul's resembled an over-iced cupcake, and the door of Number Ten was snowed in up to its top.

"Again, no one knows why London is experiencing a violent winter snowstorm in the middle of July, but we are keeping abreast of the situation. We are in contact with a number of government authorities via telephone, and they are under the impression that this attack is the work of terrorists, and is connected with the World Council of Ministers meeting in Whitehall today."

The Queen rolled her eyes. Not only had the man been repeating the same idiotic, meaningless words all day, but the World Council of Ministers was the most ridiculous creation of the modern world yet. These developing countries needed someone to *tell* them what to do. They were not remotely capable of governing themselves. Well, perhaps this would show them. The world needed monarchies. The world needed stable, benevolent authority, not all this rule-by-consensus poppycock.

Next to her, the Queen Mother shifted impatiently on the down-filled cushions of the sofa. In her agitation, tea sloshed untidily out of her china cup as it rattled in the saucer. "If you ask me, as soon as we find out who did this, we should lob a few nukes in their direction. This cannot be allowed to continue. And on Saint Swithin's Day! Balmoral will be a disaster! You need to teach them a lesson, Lilibet."

"I'm afraid it's not up to me, Mum," the Queen murmured. But she did feel things were getting out of hand. She'd missed her engagement for that day—opening the Chelsea Flower Show—because she couldn't get there through the blizzard. The helicopter pilot said he couldn't fly in this weather, and her advisors had pointed out that her subjects would be unable to attend, anyway. Really, it was all a bit much. And she'd so hoped they'd be able to *improve* on the weather. . . .

• • •

Sir August glanced up at the Big Ben monitor again. How he loved the sight of the snow-packed clock. His weather, boiling round the greatest British landmark of them all! He was making history! He was invincible!!

White clouds darkened perceptibly to black as he watched, billowing bizarrely with gases, gaining mass as they rolled through the city streets. On the exterior Serpentine Island monitor, he could see the transmitter against the swirling sky, and hear it bleeping cheerfully. *Good on,* he thought, and began to laugh, enjoying himself.

" 'Now does my project gather to a head.' It's . . . *time!*"

On his monitors, he watched the beautiful violence devastating the city. Beneath a violent sky positively crackling with energy, he saw London in apocalypse. Churches were buried up to their spires in snow; Gothic towers vanished. The snow was blowing too hard and fast for anyone to clear it up, even if they could tunnel out of their doors or garages somehow. Buses, taxis and cars had long since been buried. The Underground may have been running, but it would do no good; all of the entrances and exits would have been long since sealed by walls of snow.

Sir August sighed. The city was so beautiful with all its grit and soot covered by his white blanket. And all the antlike scurrying about had been brought to a halt. Everything but the wind and snow was perfectly still, like Christmas Day. And unless the ministers agreed to his terms, it would remain Christmas Day forever.

He put his clock up to his ear and smiled, a tear rolling down his cheek. He was master of the greatest city in the world.

• • •

Emma pushed out the metal grille that separated her from the tower platform, hearing it crash once against the metal tower as it was swept into oblivion. *There!* she told herself. If she could crawl through that claustrophobic tube, and at this height, she could do anything. She crawled through the hatch and grabbed hold of the platform on the tower, her fingers coiling round it. Now she hung over the void, with the glass bubble far, far below.

"Oooooooooh."

She forced herself to focus on the miniature control pod, the baby glass bubble she and Steed had seen from above. "Ah," she said. That was her destination. The pod was some twenty yards away, suspended over space, and attached to the side of the tower by four angled steel rods. The steel joists strained continuously in the throes of the storm, threatening to give way.

It couldn't have been easy, she thought. *Oh, no.*

Swinging herself up, and trying not to look at the view below, Emma put her left foot on one of the thin steel rods, and pulled it back again. The metal rod was crackling with energy, like a lightning rod.

But it had to be done. Emma set out with determination, hand over hand, along the steel tightrope, dangling over the sheer drop. Electric storms crackled all round her, and she hoped that somehow, miraculously, this piece of steel would not ground any of them. The steel rod was thin on the top, no wider than a quarter of an inch, with sharply cut edges that bit into her hands as she hung from it. Halfway to the pod, with the controls firmly in her sights, she swung her feet up, crossing her ankles above the rod, and traveled using both hands and feet. It was a bit easier on her hands. . . .

The rod started to vibrate and sway. High winds swept through the room, whistling eerily, and buffeting everything. *It's begun,* Emma thought as she clung to the piece of metal. The wind meant that soon it would be too late. As she swung, she saw something dark further down the rod. She did a double take as she saw Bailey, Sir August's goon, crawling down the angled rod toward her in his black polo shirt.

Just what I needed. A bit of adversity.

Emma inched onwards, her arms and legs crying out. She took her mind off of them by watching Bailey, who was faring no better than she. He had made considerable progress toward her, a nasty sneer visible on his face, when he became too hasty and slipped. Just what she expected from a hooligan.

Unfortunately, as she watched he caught himself with his hands and hung for only a moment before pulling himself back up onto the rod. Then, to her surprise, he actually stood atop it, extending his arms to keep his balance. Surely he would fall, she thought, especially the way the rod was rocking in the blast of the storms. But he came with renewed menace, and was now a mere two yards away.

She had an idea. As Bailey approached, she paused. Then she dropped her foothold again, dangling over the void by her hands. With Bailey in the picture, and with the exertion of creeping along the wire, her hands had become slippery with sweat. *Damn and blast!* She thought of releasing one hand at a time to wipe them on her suit, but didn't fancy hanging from one hand. Her grip was tight, but her hands were cramping from their ordeal. She wasn't sure how much longer she could hang on.

Ping! One of the other rods snapped like a whiplash, narrowly missing her as she flinched. Bailey didn't even seem to notice as he continued toward her, bending over now more cautiously, using both hands and feet. Now mere inches away, four inches to be precise, Emma thought, he was coming toward her hands as if to stamp on them.

Can't have that, she thought, and prepared for extreme measures. She flexed her muscles and felt her adrenaline surge as she launched into a double-legged kick—her specialty—that neatly put her boots smack into Bailey's stomach. Considerable force was delivered, and Bailey flew back against the rod, grasping for a handhold and finding it as he slid off the slim metal surface. He swung himself up again, tottering, winded, gripping the rod with both hands and feet as Emma hung once again by her hands.

She pulled herself up and straddled it, while Bailey, evidently much recovered, tried to punch and kick her. Aha! She had him now, she thought, as she saw the exposed back of his neck. Taking a huge risk, she let go with her right hand and *smack!* hit him with her best karate chop on the back of the neck. He leaned wildly, thrown off balance, and nearly tumbled off the rod. She watched him struggle to regain his equilibrium, but he finally faltered, toppling over in a deathly dive. His bloodcurdling scream faded as he plummeted downward, echoing remotely in the distance below.

"Poor boy. No head for heights," Emma grunted as she hauled herself the final two yards to the pod. She noticed that the steel supports were almost shot, their seams with the glass pod cracking. They were nearly history, creaking and swaying like a few old pieces of wood. Lightning flashed below as Emma clambered through the round opening into the pod, climbed into the seat behind the controls, and quickly flipped the switch that she knew would shut down Sir August's storms.

"Not a moment too soon," she said to herself, as the storms faltered. The lightning, wind, and rumbling quieted; in fact, she noticed the whole chamber was deathly quiet. Disturbing, somehow . . . something was wrong. . . .

She heard an odd *tick-tock*ing sound, like an old alarm clock. Where . . . ? The pod creaked, settling on the weakened rods. *Wonderful,* Emma thought, as the whole thing sank a good six inches.

Fighting the wind, Steed pulled himself down the spiral stairs in the tower after Emma left his company via the hatchway. Indeed, he did need more luck than she, for this swirling ball of energy—not at all like anything in nature, more like an electric windstorm—was whooshing upward toward him. There was no time to react. *Hang onto your hat, Steed,* he told himself. Then the wind took him, picking him up, slamming him against the sides of the stairway as he hooked his umbrella handle over the stair railing. He was now a mere pawn of Prospero. He had once been out in a windstorm with gusts of sixty miles per hour, in the famous Wiltshire windstorm of '93. This felt doubly strong, and it had only taken the sixty-mile-per-hour gusts to take out his mother's ancient elms.

As he tumbled, covering his head and bowler as best he could, he saw a door, far, far, down in the distance. It was his only hope to get out of this cyclone. . . .

Abruptly, inside the tube, the storm halted. Steed landed upside down on the stairs, in reasonable working order. He smiled, knowing Emma had succeeded, and got himself sorted out, right side up. A truly remarkable woman, he thought, and cocked his head to listen for noises. In the eerie, echoing silence, he felt oddly troubled. He could only hear the sound of his own heartbeat.

His smile faded.

Sir August stalked onto the catwalk, furious. All his plans gone awry, because of that one miserable—

well, fantastic—woman? And that ridiculous berk in the bowler!

He looked up at his fizzled storms, scowling with rage.

Then he had a magnificent idea. Slowly, a devilish grin crept across his face. "Yes, *yes!*" he cried, and raced back into the control room.

Steed frowned. There was that rumble again. But if Emma had succeeded in stopping the storm, why . . . ? Yes, there it was—faint but definitely there, echoing endlessly in the narrow tube. Now it was a mysterious roar, growing louder and louder. The metal of the stairway vibrated, throbbing, as the roar became more deafening—and threatening. Yet nothing seemed to happen. . . .

Glass started shattering somewhere, raining down on him from above. The glass of the dome, he realized in an instant, section by section. It was coming down, toward him. Quickly, he popped up his umbrella to fend off the cascading shards of glass and debris. Sounded like hail, rather, he thought.

The glass was still shattering, bit by bit, as if some furious monster were kicking out the dome on its passage to hell. A rather fitting image for Sir August, he thought. And the next moment, the furious monster that had been breaking the glass kicked him out, as well. A tremendous force struck him, knocking him through an utterly unexpected opening. The doorway he'd seen from above? Or one of Sir August's impromptu manipulations of space and structure? He found himself dangling from his opened umbrella, which had caught inside the opening, over hundreds of feet of very stormy weather.

Jolly good thing I brought my umbrella, he thought.

•   •   •

Emma assumed the worst, felt her heart harden beyond the steel it had already become. From the pod, she looked out to see Steed hanging over the vast space, buffeted by dozens of renewed storm cells. Unless he could manage a Mary Poppins number, he was done for. A pity, really . . . she had grown quite fond of him.

She flipped the switch on her console to Off, but nothing happened. Tried again . . . and again. Sir August had disabled the pod.

Hmm, she thought. *This could be it, and not just for Steed.*

Sir August, humming the "Ride of the Valkyries" with vigor, thought he heard a noise. Not just any noise; one that didn't belong to his glorious symphony of storms. He sat in the huge glass sphere below, monitoring the storm and watching, on his display screens, the greatest cyclone the world had ever seen. The swirling cloud went miles up over London, and he pitied the poor aircraft caught in its whirling vortex. Soon all of London would be nothing more than a very deadly snow sculpture.

Sir August twisted from the controls, frowning at the strange noise, only to see Steed emerging onto the catwalk from the tower. He broke into a grin and stood, advancing toward Steed as if reuniting with a long lost friend. "As I live and breathe . . . John Steed. What a horse's ass of a name. . . ."

"No time for pleasantries, Sir August. We have a score to settle."

"I see you found your brolly. Sure you're up to it, old boy?"

"Absolutely. I was going to ask the same."

Sir August fumed at the perceived insult. He advanced on Steed, pouring scorn. He couldn't let this child—this dandy, this piffling piezometer of a man—waste his time. Not tonight, the greatest night of his life.

Steed unsheathed his umbrella-sword with a swish, holding it up in the air like a pirate. Sir August immediately noticed the small crest engraved on the base of Steed's steel blade; it was the royal crest in miniature, unicorn and all, *Honi soit qui mal y pense,* with ERII prominently inscribed above it all. More than a bit presumptuous, really . . . but then, Steed struck him as the type who probably saw everything he did as a service to the Queen. The poor deluded boy . . . look where Her Majesty's Service had landed Emma's husband. Now *there* was a worthy man. . . .

"Isn't it about time you were tucked up in bed?" Sir August asked. "I can't imagine why you're here."

"Simple. I hear you enjoy a good lashing."

"I do. Frequently."

"Then allow me." Steed adopted a formal pose with his sword, as if he were one of the knights of King Arthur.

Sir August muttered, "Oh, for goodness' sake," and rolled his eyes. He half turned, concealing his hand. Instantly he brought it out again in a blur, flinging three lethal darts at Steed. The bowler boy wouldn't know what hit him, he thought, eager to be rid of the pest.

But he didn't know how to go gracefully, Sir August saw. For Steed had popped his bowler off in the nick of time, intercepting the darts with remarkable speed. The bowler looked like a pincushion, the darts bristling from it harmlessly. The boy looked crestfallen at the state of his hat. He lifted it up, inspecting it and the darts.

"You *do* look upset," Sir August said, not bothering to suppress his smile. "Punctured your bonnet?"

He saw Steed go deadly serious. *By George and the Dragon,* he thought, *he's really angry now.*

"Ruined," Steed said, glaring at him. "You'll pay for that."

"My pleasure," Sir August answered pleasantly.

"The pleasure will be all *mine*." Steed's eyes were surprisingly cold, Sir August noticed for the first time. Not unlike the Outer Hebrides in January.

Sir August picked up his staff. He didn't have time for much more of this. John Steed could be so tiresome. Thrusting the silver shaft against a red lever in the control booth, he flipped the switch up, to the On position. A low growl came from the huge glass bubble, and grew in ferocity by the second. Around them, new storms began to develop in size and intensity.

"Surprise," he said quietly to Steed.

The noise increased drastically, to deafening proportions, as Sir August, the sharp tip of his staff gleaming in the lightning, advanced on Steed.

En garde, little chappie, Sir August thought. He'd have no trouble dispatching this clotheshorse. He closed on Steed, who advanced toward him, oddly unafraid. Their eyes locked as they stepped closer, then closer still. With satisfaction, Sir August thought of the red countdown numbers spinning inexorably toward zero as the blade of his weapon clinked against Steed's at last.

They began to fight in earnest. Sir August noticed that Steed didn't fall into any of the traps of less experienced swordsmen. For one, he didn't try to rush things. He showed signs of being a classical warrior, like himself. Sir August relished a fight with a worthy adversary.

Their weapons clashed rhythmically as they moved up the catwalk, down, and back again, stepping lightly. The challenge of the duel was enhanced by the need to duck the spinning, crackling fireballs growing all around them. Sir August reflected that Saint Elmo's fire was one of the more exotic weather events created by the antimatter. As their swords met again and again, Sir August

thought that Steed's toothpick of a sword wasn't going
to do him much good against the Silver Shaft. The Shaft
had never let him down.

Grudgingly, Sir August said, "Not bad, for a beginner."

"I'm not one to boast, Sir August."

"Hmm . . . modest. And much to be modest about."

A bolt of lightning unleashed its power just behind
Steed. Maybe the weather would get him first, Sir August thought, ever the optimist. The acrid odor of the
lightning was all around them. Ah, the smell of weather.
Sir August rejoiced; he was in his element.

Inside the little pod, ever so delicately suspended over the
screaming, crackling void, Emma ducked toward the rear
of the appendage as she heard a *boooiiiiiinnnnnnnggggg!*
She knew that sound; one of the steel rods flexing. Another rod had given up the ghost, flying free as the wind
and abuse finally became too much for it. Diving as far as
she could away from the control board, she covered her
head with her arms as the rod slammed into the glass of
the pod, propelled by screaming wind. The glass exploded, and the rod bounced away into oblivion.

Exposed to the elements, Emma hung on as the wind
threatened to blow her right out of the pod. Lightning
raged now, continuously, where her head had been moments ago. She was forced to crawl along the floor to
reach the controls. The steel joists screamed as the metal
sheared and bent. She looked up at the timer racing
backwards . . . she had precisely fifty-nine seconds left
to save them all. No pressure . . .

Emma peered out over the edge, hanging onto the
built-in control board, and saw the huge glass sphere below. As she watched, a stupendous crackle of energy
built, then a brilliant flash shot through the air as a
jagged bolt of lightning connected two angry and highly

visible storm cells, hundreds of yards apart. The storm howled fiercely, buffeting the pod and bouncing it back and forth, up and down, like a carnival ride. Deafening thunder echoed round her as she reached up, groping for the control panel while hanging on for her life.

CHAPTER TWENTY-FOUR

*. . . ebbing men indeed, most often, do so near the
bottom run by their own fear or sloth.*

The Tempest, *William Shakespeare*

It wasn't Steed who picked up the pace. Sir August decided it was time to show this pretty boy what a fight
really was. Leaving courtesy behind, Sir August went
for the jugular, slashing and thrusting as well as spar-
ring. Steed proved to be surprisingly agile, dodging his
thrusts, even making some quite daring moves himself.
But Sir August wasn't worried.

Tick-tack-tick . . . the tempo of the fight increased by
the moment, in keeping with the development of the
storms around them. The wind howled now, the roar
deafening, as the wind beat at them mercilessly. Lightning and its cousin, the round, luminous electrical discharge called the corposant, now flamed and crashed all
around, but there was no dodging it. It went where it
willed.

Sir August retreated momentarily, dancing backward,

and Steed passed him on the catwalk. Never one to miss an opportunity to cheat, Sir August thrust a glancing blow at Steed as the boy moved round him. The cheating blow pushed Steed back; he nearly stumbled, but recovered his feet the next instant.

Steed's eyes acknowledged the deception, and Sir August was suddenly beset by a flurry of aggressive thrusts that let him know he wasn't going to get off as easily as he'd thought. By all that was barometric, the boy knew his swordfighting.

But Sir August had a few tricks up his sleeve yet. He forced Steed up from the gantry into the stairwell, and on up the stairs. Sir August met Steed's eyes as they advanced upward, his own mad eyes gleaming as he began to twirl his staff with blinding speed. It looked more like a rotating fan, blurring as he wielded it up and down, back and forth. It would be child's play to knock Steed's sword from his hand.

But Steed counterattacked, forcing Sir August back down the stairs even as he continued to whirl the staff.

"Impressive, Sir August." Steed had to yell with all his might to be heard over the raging wind and crashing thunder. "A man of rare talents. Such skill . . . dedication . . . utter lunacy."

"I get the job done. You think I'm mad?" Sir August found this amusing.

"I'd settle for 'evil.' Let's not quibble."

Tick-tack-tick.

"All great men have to decide," Sir August shouted. "Master? Or slave? Ever since I was a child, when Nana taught me the naming of the clouds . . ."

"Ah . . . something nasty in the nursery."

"Oh, yes," Sir August said. "Blame it on Nana."

Steed shook his head. "Poor teddy must've suffered terribly."

Tick-tack-tick-tack-tick.

"Too sentimental, Steed, that's your problem. Small

minds do small things. You and your minions at the Ministry . . . pygmies! Fools! Say goodbye to it all—summer, autumn, winter—"

"Some things are worth fighting for," Steed called. "An English spring? Sad to lose it. . . ."

"Well, old boy. I hope you're a good loser." Sir August suddenly kicked out at Steed, who lost his balance but quickly regained momentum as Sir August rushed at him, raining down blows with his staff. To Sir August's surprise, they were all neatly intercepted with that little bit of tinfoil Steed called a weapon. And that absurd umbrella handle . . . it was too pitiful by half.

"Hardly playing by the rules, Sir August."

"Rules are made to be broken."

"I should have guessed."

Sir August slashed out at Steed's legs, forcing him to jump up and lose his balance. He fell, balancing over the edge of the precipitous stairway down. One glance downward seemed to strengthen Steed's resolve, Sir August noticed as he advanced on the boy to capitalize on his distress. But to Sir August's utter amazement, Steed leaped back onto his feet and thrust at Sir August's heart. The older man only narrowly dodged the attack, and had to step backwards, which made him just a wee bit angry. He narrowed his eyes.

He would finish this horseplay—now.

Emma was on her knees on the floor of what remained of the pod, ready to delve into the digital innards of Sir August's computer system. She hoped that Sir August's system had been organized along similar lines to the Prospero Program's. Emma popped her head up long enough to key in her request for a map of the electrics, then ducked down again, away from the lightning. The pod was tossing about like a leaf in Sir August's crazy network of wind and electrical storms. When she popped up again a moment later, the map was there before her on the screen. He hadn't even modified the commands Prospero used to access its own map. She smiled and took a good hard look at the screen, memorizing the structure and form of the facility.

Dodging a lightning bolt that zigged directly into the pod, she grabbed the keyboard and slunk back onto the floor. Keyboard in her lap, she punched in the commands that would give her the coordinates for Sir August's ultimate storm. The map coordinates appeared on the screen; the lines converged on Parliament Square and Big Ben. A series of commands appeared on the screen: "ANTI-MATTER FISSION ON." "DISCONNECTION PROCESS: REVEAL CODES." Lines of eighteen-digit codes scrolled up the screen. Aha. She punched in another command, and up came the words she longed to see: "MANUAL OVERRIDE." But those lovely words were soon followed by two more that were far less pleasing: "PLEASE WAIT." Sighing, Emma obeyed. She got her head back down and sheltered under the computer table as the pod swayed and moaned. It listed significantly to starboard now. . . .

Emma popped her head up to check for a response from the computer, and was rewarded with a circuit diagram revealing a spaghetti tangle of wires. She grinned. She was almost there.

The duel between Steed and Sir August had reached the point of all-out war. They both knew that they would fight to the death, and Sir August redoubled his attack. Steed had angered him by swishing past to get away from the stairwell. They had effectively switched sides, with Steed now in the stronger position, and Sir August with his back to the catwalk. *Time to send the boy home,* Sir August thought, brandishing the staff in Steed's face. He forced him backward along the high catwalk.

The old man might be crazy, thought Steed, *but he knows how to fight. Even if he does cheat occasionally.*

Tick-tack-tick-tack-tick-tack-wham! Steed defended against Sir August, then slammed the steel fire door between the stairwell and the catwalk into Sir August's face. The older man, humiliated but only slightly stunned, emerged from behind the door full of resolve. Steed had no idea who he was fighting. . . .

Their eyes locked. Steed saw that his opponent was deadly serious now, perhaps roughly the way he himself had felt when his bowler had been ruined. Their weapons clashed in a blur, the noise utterly overwhelmed by the roaring of the ever-intensifying storm around them. Steed pressed home a momentary advantage when Sir August glanced toward the control board. With a burst of inspired thrusts, he forced Sir August back. *Surely,* Steed thought, *the man hadn't hoped to . . .*

To his surprise, Sir August turned suddenly, moving his shoulder in toward Steed. In a lightning-fast move, he flicked his blasted staff and *cling!* knocked Steed's sword clear out of his hands. Steed watched with alarm as his rosewood-handled weapon fell into the void, vanishing into . . . was it water bubbling down there now?

Quickly refocusing on Sir August, he saw the man had scented victory. Viciously, relentlessly, with blow after blow—first connecting with his shoulder, next his arm, then his rib cage—he whacked Steed down onto the steel catwalk.

This could get ugly, Steed thought, as the man whipped at him now with the razor-sharp point. The point came at him again and again, slicing his Trubshaw's waistcoat, piercing right through his suit coat and Turnbull & Asser dress shirt to his skin. A muscle in his jaw twitched as he received the wound, but he would never allow Sir August—or anyone—to see more than that. Steed, scuttling backwards on the catwalk away from the blade, finally found himself backed into a corner outside the control room. He'd found before that this could be a position of strength.

Gathering all his energy, he coiled, then sprang out of the corner, entirely focused on grabbing the staff. He didn't even see Sir August as his hands reached out and closed round the silver cylinder. Now he faced Sir August eye to eye, grappling over the weapon, all four of their hands on it. Grimly determined, Steed pushed the staff back toward Sir August, forcing the man to back up. He was winning until Sir August delivered a deft punch, right over the staff, to his nose. His *nose*! The Steed pride and joy.

Momentarily stunned, Steed lost ground until he took one hand off the staff and presented his own hard right to the jaw. Sir August had no way of knowing he had boxed for Oxford. He'd be sorry he'd opened that particular Pandora's box.

Sir August reeled from the blow, but recovered with surprising rapidity. Before Steed could reattach his right hand to the staff, Sir August wrested it away and *bam!* brought it down hard on Steed's head.

Steed felt the impact, heard the empty-coconut sound of a bad blow. He felt himself falling, falling, endlessly down . . . hoping he'd fall into the water and miss the . . .

With brutal force resulting from his considerable momentum, Steed crashed, flat on his back, onto the lower catwalk. He stared straight upward for a moment, saw Sir August above him, and then he saw no more.

Emma held her breath as she saw Steed fall. *If only I could have managed it sooner,* she thought, tortured. The pod rocked and rolled as she finally got the wires poised to connect. She took two in her left hand, one in her right. Frowning, she tried to remember which was which from the diagram, now off the screen. There was no *time*!

"Red . . . or was it black?"

Sir August practically danced down the stairwell to the lower catwalk, where he advanced to the stunned Steed. Holding his staff aloft, he stood over the boy, who looked utterly dazed. Who knew? A man's back could be broken in a fall like that. He leaned down and watched as Steed blinked, widening his eyes and then squinting as if trying to focus. He rolled his head back and forth slowly as if it helped him endure the pain. . . .

Jolly good fun, this. Sir August smiled and stood. He raised his staff high into the heavens as if it were Merlin's wand. Relishing Steed's imminent and delicious demise, he moved down the gantry. He had the perfect Shakespeare quote for this moment. . . .

Sir August cleared his throat and began. " 'We are such stuff as dreams are made on; and our little life is rounded with a sleep. . . .' " He cast a glance down at Steed, whose eyes were open, staring at him glassily, lips parted. "Say good night, old boy."

As he grasped the staff with both hands to bring it down for the ultimate blow, Sir August saw Steed's head roll sideways, as if to avoid the blow. *Pitiful creature*, he thought with disdain. But to his surprise, Steed rolled over and reached under the edge of the catwalk, where heavy electrical cables hung. As he peered round to see, he saw Steed deftly unhooking the rosewood handle of his umbrella from one of the cables. John Steed seemed to lead a charmed existence . . . though not, of course, as charmed as his own.

He found himself looking at Steed's ridiculous umbrella sword, rising in front of Steed as the boy got to his feet. He brought his staff down, but Steed was able to thwart the blow, though Sir August noted he was much the worse for wear. This would be easy.

Feeling the pod sag dangerously, knowing that the rods couldn't hold it much longer, Emma took a chance— "Here goes . . . eeny-meeny-miny . . ."—and brought two wires together. Red and black. *Craaacccckkkkk!* A huge surge of energy leapt out. Emma jumped back.

Hmm . . . lucky guess.

Steed knew he had gained the advantage; he felt it. The little fall he'd taken hadn't helped, but Sir August obviously hadn't been expecting him to make a comeback from the floor of the catwalk. And he *was* all right—bit of a buzzing in his head, or was that part of the storm? Sir August knew how to cook up one hell of a storm, that was certain.

Like twin dervishes, they went at it again, weapons blurring into a silver cloud between them. Steed forced Sir August's staff up, held it up and away with his sword, then without ceremony plunged his blade into Sir August's heart.

Steed saw the maniac stop dead in his tracks, well, *almost* dead—his staff raised high in his right hand. In agony, disbelieving, Sir August stared at Steed.

"Sir, I am vexed—"

Cracccckkkk! One of his beloved balls of Saint Elmo's fire knocked him back, seeming to build a thick, intense little storm around Sir August. A spectacular specimen of a lightning bolt, evidently just aching to join the party, zapped down, connecting with the staff in Sir August's raised hand. *A veritable lightning rod,* Steed thought as he watched the bolt travel through Sir August's body, holding him in a deadly embrace.

Positively electrifying performance, Steed thought.

Sir August screamed out one last time, still racked by the wild flow of natural energy, until his brain was—well—fried. Steed watched as the madman was sucked backward off the catwalk into the vortex, spinning away into the storm of his own making.

"Well, he made his bed, he can lie in it," Steed said, straightening his lapels. Suddenly, he heard a frightful racket of screaming metal and the loud *zzzzzzzt!* of high voltage discharge, audible even above the general clamor of the storm.

His head jerked up to Emma's pod, which was exploding in a tragic bloom of electric sparks and smoke. He saw her leap away from the explosion, and as the floor began to fall away beneath her, she stood, arched her long limbs and back and dived over the side, into the maelstrom. His head swiveled as he watched her sail through space, executing a perfect "ten" swan dive. Energy crackled round her in an electric slipstream as she slid smoothly into the water below, through flames floating on the water.

Steed's head jerked up once again as he heard a second ominous cracking sound from the pod. It broke loose from the tower, tumbling after Emma into the fiery water.

At a run, Steed made for the stairway down.

Outside, the storms began to clear. The giant cyclone hovering over Big Ben started to dissipate, breaking up into gentle cirrus wisps. The sparkling snow dwindled, then stopped completely, and bright sunlight broke through the clouds. The iced wedding-cake spire of Saint Bride's Church on Fleet Street began to drip; the heavy skullcap of melting snow slid off the dome of Saint Paul's.

The Queen stepped out onto her private balcony and surveyed the scene with satisfaction. It looked as if they'd be going to Balmoral after all, and since today was ending with fine weather, the next forty days might be fine as well.

But she'd learned something from this day; perhaps, when they'd got the experimental weather facility going again, she could arrange for a snow day like this now and again—the Queen's privilege, you know. They couldn't expect her to carry on in this thankless job without a few perquisites.

At last she'd found an honorable way to dodge those most onerous of responsibilities. She didn't mind the Chelsea Flower Show; quite looked forward to it, in fact. But there were a few public appearances she *could* do without. . . .

And, if her experts could now control the weather, perhaps they could ensure fair-weather sailing wherever the royal yacht cruised. They had a brief holiday scheduled for September in the Caribbean. . . .

She smiled and gazed out at the rapidly melting snow.

As Steed ran along the lower catwalk, distraught, he saw no sign of Emma. Leaning out over the water, he grabbed onto a vertical beam for support and surveyed the roiling waves. It would be a miracle if she survived, he told himself. The fall, the flames, the electricity— and who knew what was beneath the surface of that water . . .

Then, to his amazement, directly before him in the swells, Emma's head popped up. He heard a desperate, involuntary wheeze as she sucked in air, bobbing among the flames on the water. He could hear her gasping for breath, frantic to fill her lungs, but coughing in the smoke. Steed lowered himself under the catwalk, using the framework that suspended it to climb down to the water. He reached out to her, grabbed a handful of the catsuit where it was unzipped on her chest, and pulled her from the water. He tossed her over his right shoulder, and with one arm wrapped round her legs, climbed up to safety with her. As he reached the surface of the catwalk, he lifted her off his shoulder, lowering her gently onto the perforated metal.

He knelt over her, watching her cough and breathe. "Mrs. Peel."

"What . . . kept you?" She looked into his eyes, and a smile spread over her wet face, all the way up to, and including, her eyes. He basked in the smile and gave her one of his own.

She got to her feet, Steed's solicitous hand under her elbow. *Click-click!* They wheeled as they heard the ominous mechanical sound from the control room, as if gears were shifting.

Emma frowned. "Sounds . . . as if the program has reconfigured," she said. They heard a *beeep!* And then the distressing news from the computer's synthesized voice: "Autodestruct, ten seconds." The message flashed behind Emma in the control room on the monitor. A new set of numbers began to run backwards.

"You must be joking," said Emma, incredulous.

They looked at each other, eyes wide.

"And I thought you had it all under control," Steed said.

Sir August's little alarm clock *tick-tock*ed disturbingly, as the synthesized Emma voice calmly intoned, "Nine, eight, seven . . ."

Inside Prospero's cave, the countdown continued. "Three, two, one . . ."

A blast like a nuclear explosion shook the underground headquarters, traveling down the vast inner chamber with a *whoooooossshshhhh!* The firestorm swept through the Doric-columned car park–like space and through the endless corridors of Sir August's ill-fated domain.

The blast continued right up through the phone box lift chamber, rocketing skyward, first making the Serpentine ripple and the leaves on the trees shake. Rumbling from far beneath the earth, the blast reached the surface. A fireball the size of Bedford Square belched out of the water, spewing debris up into the sky, leaving a mushroom plume of smoke crackling with static electricity. The whole mess ascended into the clouds, where slowly, colors resembling the aurora borealis surged and swirled through the sky, illuminating the trails of the fireball in a garish display.

The Queen was having her evening meal with Prince Philip when she heard the blast. Assuming it was the Irish Republican Army flexing its muscles again, she groaned and closed her copy of *Corgi World*. "Would you excuse me for a moment, please," she said to Prince Philip, and went to the window, standing well back as the bodyguards had instructed her. Prince Philip didn't even seem to notice; he was perusing a copy of his beloved *Horse and Hound*.

As she stood scanning her domain, she marveled at the number of disasters that could occur in a single day, fully prepared to see smoke rising from some unfortunate target of the IRA. But as she peered out the window, she saw that it was an ordinary summer evening in London: gentle sunset colors blending into a light blue sky scattered with clouds. Thank goodness the weather had cleared! She saw no smoke, speeding ambulances, or panda cars, and reached a decision.

"Must've been daydreaming," she said.

CHAPTER TWENTY-FIVE

The time 'twixt six and now must by us both be spent most preciously.

The Tempest, *William Shakespeare*

Deep in the bowels of the Ministry, Brenda stared out the window at the Thames. Above ground, she knew, it would be reflecting the glorious colors of the late summer sunset, now that the weather had cleared. The emergency was over, evidently—she'd known John would save the day—but what a loss! And Emma Peel, too . . . to think that she'd actually *wished* her out of the picture earlier. She felt so ashamed.

She wrung her hands as she watched the murky water flow past. Mother had instructed her to order macaroons, cakes and tea—at this hour! She'd hardly known what to make of Mother's insensitivity to the fact that John hadn't returned, though it was true that he had a way of popping up, unscathed, after legendary disasters. . . .

She fought back tears as she heard Mother on the hotline to the PM.

"Yes, sir. Confirm reports the storm is dropping. . . . Spot of internal trouble. I took a firm grip. One or two casualties. No word from our people yet. . . . Thank you, sir."

He put the phone down, and turned to Brenda. "Pity about Steed and Mrs. Peel," he said.

"Missing in action?" she said.

"Better send out a search party. You never can tell." Brenda raced to the telephone.

Had Brenda not turned away from the window to effect a rescue for Steed, she would have seen a most remarkable sight. For a huge white bubble floated along past the Ministry picture window on its way up through the River Thames. Just past the Ministry, the bubble disturbed the glassy surface of the water as it popped up, then rolled over, floating downstream with the current.

Inside the BROLLY emergency escape pod, Emma nestled closer to Steed.

"The owl and the pussycat went to sea . . ." he began.

". . . In a beautiful pea-green boat."

"A fine night, Mrs. Peel. Just a bit chilly. I think we deserve some champagne. . . ."

Sergei Ivanovich strode into the pleasant London evening. There was no car waiting; anything could have happened to his chauffeur. Perhaps he'd frozen to death. No matter; he knew his own way to the Savoy well enough by now. He could hardly wait to reach the security of his room, where he would telephone his homeland and tell them that he, now chairman of the World Council of Ministers, had solved the global weather crisis. He would explain that it had taken tremendous negotiating skill against one of the world's most insidious villains to achieve this. While the other ministers had whimpered and whined, he alone had prevailed, refusing to knuckle under to the demands of a madman. The world could rest, safe in the knowledge that he, Sergei Ivanovich, was in charge.

Yes, this would do nicely. He would no longer have to worry about his position at home. In fact, perhaps he would make a gesture of magnanimity to the British, so great was his stature now. He had always wanted to meet the Queen personally.

Sergei beamed as he neared the Savoy. Ah, the Thames was lovely. And soon he would be having a lovely English dinner—why people complained about English food, he could never understand—and some fine Russian vodka.

Steed basked in the eighty-degree paradise of his rooftop garden, now and then opening his eyes long enough to cast a glance at Emma. She was fetchingly attired in sunglasses, a revealing halter top, nothing around her midriff whatever, and a nearly nonexistent skirt—all in the most outrageous lime green. Mother, who had joined them for a brief sun-worshipping holiday, wore his usual black trousers, but with a wildly exotic tropical print shirt that had been given him as a gift. Steed himself wore short pants and a golf shirt; most daring for him. The three of them were lined up in lounge chairs like tourists on a beach in Mallorca.

Emma sighed with contentment, then spoke. "I don't recall London being this warm, Steed."

He gazed off into the fogbound city surrounding their bit of blue sky. "Wonderland Weather, Mrs. Peel. The latest thing. I made an early booking."

Steed heard the champagne bottle rattling about in the ice, and looked over to see Mother preparing to open it. With practiced skill he removed the wire and wrapping, and Steed heard the delicate *pop* that promised the tickle of toasty bubbles.

"Champagne?" Mother offered, holding out a glass in one hand and lifting the bottle in the other.

"Please," said Emma.

"Of course," said Steed.

"A toast"—Mother raised his glass—"to a job well done."

The three raised their glasses, clinked and then drank. The cold wine tasted heavenly, Steed thought, drunk under the hot sun.

"To a narrow escape," Emma said, looking out over London with deliberate nonchalance.

"I did have him, of course," Steed said a bit defensively.

"Did you," she said, smiling as she sipped her champers. Steed thought he detected a touch of skepticism.

He sat upright in his lounge chair and said, "Mrs. Peel, if I say I had him . . ."

"Ahem," Mother broke in. "Macaroon?"

Emma laughed, and Mother joined in, then finally Steed. Mother led them in another companionable clink of the glasses.

"Thank you, Steed," Emma said, removing her sunglasses to look at him directly. She was still smiling her clever, naughty smile.

Steed, having matched her courtesy in lowering his sunglasses, met her level gaze.

"No. Thank you, Mrs. Peel."

the avengers
the making of the movie
DAVE ROGERS

the avengers

ORIGINAL MOVIE SCREENPLAY

Don Macpherson

THE
AVENGERS
COMPANION

over [ ] colour photographs

ALAIN CARRAZÉ & JEAN-LUC PUTHEAUD

THE AVENGERS

AND ME

PATRICK MACNEE

WITH DAVE ROGERS

THE AVENGERS AND ME

By Patrick Macnee with Dave Rogers

For the first time, Patrick Macnee tells all! The behind-the-scenes secrets of the classic television series *The Avengers* are laid bare by the man who *was* John Steed. In unflinching detail, Macnee reveals the true story behind *The Avengers*, including his relationships with all four *Avengers* girls — on *and* off the set. Honor Blackman and her kinky boots, Diana Rigg as Emma Peel, Linda Thorson as Tara King, onto Joanna Lumley and *The New Avengers*, and even an appearance with Oasis, Macnee witnessed it all.

Lavishly illustrated, with many rare and previously unpublished pictures from Macnee's private collection, and with contributions by fellow *Avengers* actors, directors, producers and screenwriters, this is a unique history of the trials and triumphs of a series as popular today as when it was first screened.

'Charming... Hats off to you, sir!' — *Uncut*

'A frank, unmissable read.' — *SFX*

To order by credit card, phone 01536 763 631